LITTLE TOWN

of

DEATH-LEHEM

THE POSSUMWOOD MYSTERIES BOOK 12

HOLLY DEY

Little Town of Death-Lehem: The Possumwood Mysteries Book 12 © 2022 by Holly Dey. All rights reserved.

Black Mare Books

First Edition 2022

This is a work of fiction. Names, characters, places, brands, media, and incidents are either the product of the author's imagination or are used fictitiously. The author acknowledges the trademarked status and trademark owners of various products referenced in this work of fiction, which have been used without permission. The publication/use of these trademarks is not authorized, associated with, or sponsored by the trademark owners.

ISBN: 978-1-959008-24-8

Acknowledgements

I couldn't do this without the love and support of my wonderful family. I love you so much!

Chapter 1

"IT'S FREEZING IN here!" Primrose Corvina Donovan said. The retired homicide detective hugged herself and rubbed her arms. "I'm surprised Woody didn't come."

Officer Hiro Tran closed the door to the City Café. "He wasn't feeling well."

She sighed softly. "I was afraid of that. That last round of chemo seems to have hit him really hard."

Tran nodded solemnly.

His new bride, fresh from their tropical honeymoon, re-entered the restaurant and handed Tran a coat. "Here. I got your jacket while I was getting mine."

Thanksgiving week had ushered in a cold front, but the weather wasn't bad enough to keep many of the Possumwood denizens at home from the Black Friday sales. Houston, an hour away, offered an irresistible shopping smorgasbord for some, while others preferred the assorted big box stores in closer towns. The normally busy City Café was all but deserted.

PC glanced at the newlyweds and her thoughts strayed to warmer climes. "I want to hear all about your trip, Annie. I've never been to Jamaica before."

"It was so amazing! My favorite thing was the Rocklands Bird Sanctuary. They give you this little tube of sugar water and the hummingbirds will come sit on your hand so you can feed them.

Hiro got so many closeups, I think my mom will be painting hummingbirds for the next decade."

The detective scanned the dining area as she walked. PC had done threat assessments for so long that it was as normal for her as breathing. She never even realized she was doing it unless something popped up on her radar.

A young man, the hood of his jacket pulled up over his head, sat in the corner, scrolling on his phone. He didn't look dangerous, so much as out of place. PC noted him in her head and continued toward the large table in the center of the restaurant. At least half of Possumwood PD was there, as were Tran's mom and Annie's parents, who also happened to be PC's next-door neighbors. Well, her mother's next-door neighbors. PC had arrived last January to take care of Rose's collection of rescued farm animals while her mother was recovering from breaking her hip. Almost a year later, the detective was still there, even though Rose was getting around better with her new titanium hip than she had with the original factory install.

PC did contract work for the Possumwood Police Department from time to time and knew most of the officers in the small department. She'd even dated the chief, Elwood Wilson, decades ago in high school. Age had made him even more ornery, but at least he listened to her professional opinion. Sometimes. Sadly, he wasn't well enough to be here today to celebrate.

Tran had taken the last exam he needed for the Texas Commission on Law Enforcement Advanced Proficiency Certificate the day after he and Annie had returned from their honeymoon. As everyone who worked with him expected, he passed it with a perfect score.

The detective found a seat next to Annie's mom, Lin Youn. While Tran and Annie made their way around the table, receiving high fives and hugs, PC and Lin talked about painting, yard eggs, and Rose and her boyfriend, Terry. He was the Youns other next door neighbor. One of the servers came by to take her drink order.

"Hey, Frida. Three ice teas, please. One sweet."

"The sweet's for Annie, right?" Frida looked at the couple standing on the other side of the table.

Lin chuckled. "My daughter and her sweet tooth."

"I'll have those right up." Frida paused at another table on her way to the back.

The teas arrived so quickly PC would have believed it if someone told her there was a teleportation device installed in the café. She took a sip of the icy beverage and shivered, wondering if she should have ordered coffee instead.

At last, Tran sat down next to PC, and Annie next to him. Officer Gorman, who was typically Woody's stand-in, stood up. He raised his tea glass and said, "Guess y'all know why we're here. Our man, Tran—he's got more book learnin' than the Chief now, so raise a glass."

He took a deep draught from his plastic tumbler, then pointed a finger at Tran. "You better take good care of our dispatcher, now."

Good-natured laughter around the table turned Annie's cheeks bright red.

Frida came around and took food orders. She'd brought reinforcements this time. Esmerelda did one half of the table, while a young man PC didn't recognize refilled drinks.

Lin elbowed PC. "Is your mother practicing her singing?"

"Singing?" As far as PC was aware, Rose couldn't carry a tune in a bucket.

"Well, she tried to sign both Quon and I up for the Christmas cantata when they started practicing last month. I have no desire to get up on stage and sing." She inclined her head toward her spouse. "He's been enjoying it, though. Hardly any men, so he mostly gets his pick of parts."

PC had completely forgotten about Rose trying to recruit her offspring for the concert. Her brother, Rocky, usually worked evenings at the Azalea Manor nursing home. And Daisy… well, Daisy had her own unique vocal stylings. The choir director may not have realized what a bullet he dodged when she begged off.

"I have been really busy, so I haven't been keeping up. I believe she and Terry have been having fun going to rehearsals. Now that I think about it, I seem to recall that my nephew, Tyson, joined at the last minute. If I remember correctly, his girlfriend has a solo."

"I think he's Quon's biggest competition. I've been to some of the rehearsals, and there is a young lady with a beautiful voice."

"Well, I'll be looking forward to hearing a preview at the Christmas Tree lighting tomorrow."

"I hope everyone out hitting the sales today saves some money for the vendors there. The tree-lighting is an all-afternoon event these days. One year, they even got artificial snow."

PC rubbed her arms again. "If it gets any colder, we may have real snow."

Lin snorted. "That would be a once-in-a-lifetime event. Did you have anything for the rummage sale?"

"I was not aware there was one."

"Five of the local churches are collaborating on the cantata, so they also have a giant rummage sale, proceeds to go to help the needy during the holidays. They've pooled their holiday requests and are setting up a tree where each ornament has a child's name and what they want for Christmas. You can buy the gift for them, and they'll distribute the items the week of Christmas."

"I'll have to keep my eye out for that. And the rummage sale. I can't remember the last time I went to one of those."

"If you find one, you'll find the other. Sometimes they have some good stuff. One year, Dinah Mae Brown unearthed a set of china plates from the 1800s. She put 'em up on display at the Quenton Plantation."

PC chortled. "I can one-hundred percent believe that. Dinah Mae's like a truffle pig for antiques." The president of the Mirabella County Historical Society was not one to let an antique of any sort fall by the wayside.

The conversation was interrupted by hot plates of food, and jawing was replaced by chewing.

The detective leaned back in her chair. She couldn't quite finish the slab of Winnie Hargraves' famous chocolate pie. A nap. Cold day. Full belly. Seemed like the only reasonable thing to do next was sleep off the feast.

Motion to PC's left caught her attention. The young man in the hoodie was suddenly at their table.

"Detective Donovan? I've been looking for you for a long time."

He reached inside his jacket.

Chapter 2

CHAIRS SCRAPED ACROSS the wood floor as all the cops scrambled to their feet. Tran reached for his weapon.

PC grabbed his arm. "Wait."

The young man pulled a stained, moth-eaten teddy bear from his jacket and shucked off his hood. "I'm sorry." He looked around the table at the tense officers. "Didn't mean to cause a scene." His gaze turned back to PC. "I never forgot this."

The detective blinked several times. His face was familiar, but not. An image forced its way through the fog of memory. "Antoine?"

He nodded his head, moisture glistening on his thick lashes. "You recognize me? After twelve years… I look a lot different now."

"You do." PC opened her arms, and he stooped to grab her in a hug.

After a long moment, he let go and stepped back.

Tran's party resumed their seats.

PC gestured toward a small table for two.

Antoine pulled out a chair and sat. PC did the same.

He ran a finger along the rim of the bear's remaining button eye. "It took some digging to find out it was you."

PC smiled faintly. "You were a little kid. Just lost your mom and your dad was going to jail for the rest of his life. You deserved better than the foster system."

"I don't know how you found them, my mother's people."

"Well, your parents were both using fake identities. But when I ran your father's fingerprints… he had a long record in Baton Rouge. Nothing came up for your mother, not even a driver's license. I asked the sheriff's department about missing persons in that parish, and your mother's description kind of matched a teenager who'd gone missing about ten years before. Your grandmother had no idea she even had a grandson."

"You saved my life. Both literally and figuratively. I'm on my way home from Sam for winter break."

"You're going to college? That's fantastic!" There was suddenly some dust in PC's eye, and she blotted it.

He grinned as he nodded. "Graduating in May from the Sam Houston State College of Criminal Justice."

PC's hand flew to her mouth. "Wow. I am so proud of you. What are you going to do?"

"Well, I've already started working on applications for some larger departments. Thinking about putting one in to DPS, with an eye to making Ranger."

"Trooper Miller. Has a nice ring to it."

He grinned and looked at the table for a moment. "I have to get back on the road. Like I said, it took a while to find you. I just… I just needed to thank you for what you did for that terrified little boy all those years ago." He stood up and tucked the ragged teddy bear back into his coat. "It's my turn to be one of the helpers now."

PC also rose. She had to reach up to squeeze his shoulder. "Thank you. I'm really glad you stopped by. Merry Christmas, Antoine."

This is just about the best present I ever got.

"Merry Christmas, Detective."

"You be safe out there. And give your grandma a hug for me."

"Yes, ma'am."

The detective watched him walk out of the City Café, savoring the moment. Being a homicide detective means being the bearer of unwelcome news. Families are shattered, and even catching the killer won't put the pieces back together. She hadn't realized how much she had needed to see Antoine Miller.

"Hurry up, Primrose!" Rose scolded.

"I'm putting my shoes on, Mama." PC caught a glimpse of herself in the mirror as she straightened up. The green sweater would have to be Christmasy enough. "Alright, let's go."

The detective's terrier mix dog followed them hopefully to the door. "Sorry, Cordite. You'll have to stay and guard the house."

Rose, in a long red dress, and Terry, in a brilliant red satin waistcoat, climbed into the back seat of PC's SUV. The Possumwood tree-lighting festival had been going on all afternoon. Rose wanted to save her energy for the cantata preview performance, so they decided to leave the house a bit later. The detective hoped she had some time to do a little holiday shopping before the show—she wanted to ask Teskia Turner if she'd be able to do a custom stained-glass piece for Rose in time for Christmas. And the Biersal might have brought some of their famous pretzels to sell at the beer tent.

"Mama, break a leg. You, too, Terry." PC called after the couple as they hurried to find the choir director, Whit Bulger.

The detective took a few steps backward and bumped into someone. "Excuse me! I'm so sorry."

She turned to find herself in a one-sided conversation with a six-foot nutcracker statue. His royal blue coat and silver buttons mirrored the blue bows and silver baubles that decorated the garlands that wrapped around the gazebo supports. Potted poinsettias clustered around the base of the gazebo and sprung from the large concrete planters at the front of the park.

PC pulled out her phone to text Drew. Before she even unlocked it, he was there, holding a cheesecake-on-a-stick in one hand and about a third of a cheesecake-on-a-stick in the other. He handed her the whole one.

"Thanks." She couldn't help but grin at him. "So, what's there to see?"

"Well, you can have your picture taken with Santa, and there's a reindeer petting zoo."

PC crinkled her brow. "Not sure how Mama's critters would react if I came back smelling like a reindeer. Guinevere might bite me. I heard there was a rummage sale with a special tree, so I want to find that, but mainly, I'm looking for the stained-glass lady."

Drew linked his arm in hers. "Anything particular in mind?"

"A custom piece."

Squeezed from a mournful French horn, the notes of "What Child is This," drifted from the gazebo. The heady aromas of funnel cake and turkey legs overpowered most other festival perfumes. But PC caught a whiff of beer and nosed her way to the Biersal tent. She snagged the last pretzel and a paper cup of hot apple cider. She checked her FlitBit. The low battery light on the ersatz fitness tracker was glowing red. The detective had about twenty minutes before the cantata preview started.

She picked up the pace, scouring the vendor areas for Teskia's booth. At last, she found it. Drew moved over to admire some of the pieces on display.

"Mrs. Turner?"

The young woman smiled and gave her head a gentle nod. The metal and glass beads on her long, thin braids clicked as they collided. "That's me."

"My name is PC Donovan. I've been admiring your work for a while now. Do you do custom pieces?"

"I do."

"Do you have a minute? I'd like to run something by you, so you can give me a ballpark price and an estimated time frame. Was hoping to have it as a Christmas gift, but I realize I may have left it way too late."

"Tell me what you have in mind."

"Mama has some rescued farm animals—two donkeys and a goat, and some chickens. I was thinking of a design with them in it."

"How big?"

PC held her hands about a foot apart. "Not huge, but big enough you can recognize the animals."

Teskia nodded. "If I have all the colors and don't have to order anything, probably six to eight weeks."

"That's what I thought. It may have to be a birthday present. That's May, so plenty of time."

"Why don't you give me some photos, and I'll see what I can do. I'll have a better idea of how long it will take, and I'll be able to quote you a price."

"Thank you so much. What's the best way to get it to you?"

The artisan handed her a card. "Email it."

"Perfect! I'll get those to you tonight or tomorrow."

"Looking forward to it." Teskia turned to help another customer.

The scent of warm cinnamon and butter drifted on the air and PC breathed deeply. She scanned the booths for the source. *That's gotta be it.*

She dragged Drew to a big crimson sign that read:

Jillibella's Mexican Diner

Tacos * Burritos * Sopapillas * Churros

The owner, Jill Franco, who had gone to school with PC way back when, grinned as they approached. "Hey, girl! How're you likin' the tree lightin' ceremony?"

PC grinned back. "I'll let you know when some tree lighting actually happens. I'd like to get some sopapillas."

"I'm sorry. Sold out. Still have a couple of churros, though. I was getting ready to pack up—that's all I have left."

The detective turned to Drew. "Would you like a churro?"

"Sure. Why not?"

"Alright. I'll take two churros."

Armed with sticks of cinnamon-sugar-dipped fried dough, Drew and PC meandered toward the bandstand. They paused at various booths along the way.

Rose's friend Justice Johnson waved PC over to her mini-shop. Three bars of goat milk soap and a skein of fine white yarn sat on the table.

"Hey, PC. I saved some of that new recipe goat milk lotion for your mama." She reached under the table and retrieved a plastic bottle. "She hadn't made it by yet, and I wanted to finish packin' up."

"Thanks, Justice. I'll give it to her."

Justice began folding up her red tablecloth, so PC and Drew continued their browsing.

Handmade by Carolyn featured crocheted ornaments and Christmas themed draft-dodgers—those long-legged dolls that do the splits in front of doors to keep out cold air.

Norma Jean's Nibbles displayed red and green popcorn balls and Santa-shaped Rice Krispie treats.

Mary Grace Has Gone to the Dogs boasted an eye-popping array of holiday dog sweaters and matching accessories. PC paused, her eyes on a blue and gold Nordic Faire Isle knit with reindeer and a lighthouse, but a man snatched it up before she could get near it.

The detective sighed, they moved on to *Beverly's Beverages*. Custom tea blends made with home-grown herbs and spices were on offer there.

Glass jars of *Heidi's Honey* were prominently on display as well. In fact, the strong smell of honey was almost overpowering. Then she noticed a broken jar of it in the trash.

A woman wearing beaded Santa earrings and a Christmas sweater patterned with a dizzying array of holiday presents stepped into the tent, accompanied by another woman similar in age, who wore a red sweater bearing the single word Noel repeated in various fonts and sizes.

"I've told you, Susan, I never, ever get honey at the grocery store. Most of that stuff is counterfeit."

Susan scrunched up her face. "Counterfeit honey? What are you talking about? Honey is honey."

The Present Lady shook her head "*Unnh uh uh.* A lot of these big brands get their honey from China in bulk and just repackage it. It's loaded with corn syrup or molasses, and who knows what else? That's why it's so cheap, and cheap honey ain't real honey. Nope." She pointed to the display of *Heidi's Honey*. "I only ever buy my honey at the farmer's market."

She put three jars of honey on the table and whipped out a platinum Amex. Her companion bought one container.

PC bought a jar of dark honey, a box of *Deep Sleep* tea for herself, and a box of *Nice on Ice* for Rose. Drew bought two boxes of *Better Than Pumpkin Spice*.

"You have to try this." He waved one of the boxes at her before dropping it back in the bag. "Best breakfast tea ever."

They continued to drift toward the gazebo until Drew stopped dead.

PC looked around. Nothing interesting stood out. "What?"

Drew looked up and her eyes followed his. Overhead, a ball of bright green leaves sprouted from a bare branch.

He brought his gaze back to her. "Mistletoe."

"How about that?"

Drew leaned toward her, and PC closed her eyes.

"There y'all are!" Daisy shouted. "Mama and Ty's about to go on!"

They pulled away from each other like guilty teenagers.

Should I thank Daisy later or scold her? Once a line is crossed…

PC and Drew hurried toward PC's sister. The crowd was thickening around the gazebo, but Daisy jostled her way to the front, dragging the other two behind her and leaving a trail of apologies. The cantata group was entering the gazebo as the trio found a good spot in the audience.

After all of the practices, the cantata extravaganza was making its debut. The pastor of the Possumwood First Methodist Church, Martha Henry, introduced the organist—Lydia Maison—while the singers found their places. Lydia was the same one who played at Tran and Annie's wedding. Reverend Thomas Wholt, of St. Mark's Episcopal Church, hung a banner from the railing of the gazebo with the vital details of the cantata, along with all the churches' social media handles.

Daisy gave a single nod. "He done a real good job with that. Does graphic designin' on the side, you see. Did some ads for Karla's Kurls. Had more customers that week than we could handle."

A man in a charcoal-grey suit and complicated coiffure took a microphone and stepped to the front of the Gazebo. "Good evening, Possumwood!"

The crowd returned a patchy response.

"I said, good evening, Possumwood!"

Realizing the show was not going on without a response, the crowd obliged.

He beamed. "For those of you who do not know me, I am the *Reverend* Richard Costas. I have taken over shepherding the flock at Justice Avenue Baptist Church. I am so proud of my colleagues for stepping up to the plate. This has truly been a group effort. You folks are welcome to worship with us at any time, but I am so pleased to welcome you all to our house in two weeks to witness this glorious spectacle.

"Now, you all have already met Reverend Henry—we love her so much! Please give a round of applause for Pastor Wholt for all of his hard work on our announcements and programs." He gestured toward the Episcopalian minister, who bowed slightly as the audience clapped. He was a slender man who sported an ugly bruise on his left cheekbone.

As the applause faded, Costas spoke again. "Nobody. And I mean no*body* has worked as hard as Reverend Steve Anders. Can I get a shout-out for Justice Lutheran?" Costas paused for half a second. "He is in charge of organizing the refreshments. There will be some special treats in store, let me tell you."

Reverend Anders raised his hand and grinned. "We're going to be making enough gingerbread for the whole town, so if anybody knows where we can buy molasses in bulk, message me." He chuckled and turned his head back toward Costas.

"Heidi's Honey!" came a voice from the crowd.

Anders blushed. "Yes. Well. I'll have to ask, next time I see her." He clutched his left wrist with his right hand, closing himself off, and took a step backward.

Once the spotlight was back on Costas, he gestured dramatically with his free arm. "Now I am going to hand this microphone over to Father. Xavier. Benaviiiiiides."

He sounds like he's announcing a wrestling match.

Father Benavides took the mic and surveyed the crowd, a faint smile curling his lips. He nodded to a few people in the audience. The man was shorter and rounder than average, but he was attractive in the same way as a grandparent is to a grandchild. "Thank you, Reverend Costas. St. Lucia's is pleased to have our choir director, Whit Bulger, as the choir director for the cantata. He has worked so hard to bring out the best in these singers. And I hope he is as inspiring to you as he is to them."

"*Huh.* I had no idea he was musically inclined." Drew rubbed his chin.

"Who is he?" PC whispered back.

"Owns City Bail Bonds."

A beast of a man stepped from behind the singers. He was every bit of six foot four, maybe taller, and built like a bull. His head was shaved, but blond stubble occasionally caught the light. A tattoo peeked out of the edge of his collar, but there wasn't enough showing to tell what it was. PC recognized him as Woody's motorcycle riding buddy, but she'd only met him in passing.

"Evenin' y'all." He spoke in a velvety baritone. "We're going to give you a little preview tonight to whet your appetite for our upcoming performance at the Christmas cantata."

He turned and faced the choir. The song wasn't one PC recognized, but she found herself bobbing her head to the music. Tenor, soprano, alto, and baritone voices all interlaced and separated, weaving an intricate web of sound.

The smell of wood smoke drifted over the crowd.

Probably just the Brisk Rib Barbecue extinguishing their pit and packing up.

Until the singers, one by one, stopped singing.

"Fire!" someone shouted at the back of the crowd.

Chapter 3

PC TURNED. THROUGH the leaves of the rose hedge that surrounded *Happily Ever Afters*, orange flames licked the sky. Pale grey smoke billowed into the darkening evening.

"Sorry, y'all! Fire Department. I have to get over there!" Whit Bulger vaulted over the railing of the gazebo and sprinted toward the fire.

Cell phones buzzed and chirped throughout the crowd and the choir. The Possumwood Volunteer Fire Department was being summoned.

Simone and Caitlyn. "Drew, we have to get to the Afters!" The B&B owners lived on the ground floor of the property.

He grabbed her hand, and they pushed their way through the crowd, which churned around them like a stepped-on fire ant bed. The pair crossed Main Street and stood at the locked gate to *Happily Ever Afters*, the popular bed & breakfast and wedding venue, peering through the wrought iron bars.

"It's not the Afters," Drew said.

"You're right. What is it?"

They moved down the sidewalk and made a left onto the paved utility easement that ran between the Afters and the buildings next to it.

Drew craned his neck toward the conflagration. "I think it's the old caretaker's cottage that's next to the Afters."

They hurried toward the abandoned building. PC had seen it several times in passing. "Is this part of the Afters?"

Drew shook his head in time with his footfalls. "Not anymore. Used to belong to the original estate, but it had been split up long before Simone and Caitlyn purchased the house."

They were now as close as PC was willing to get. She didn't want to get under the firefighters' feet, but she got a good view of the building. Though neglected, the cottage had been well-constructed with fieldstone and local cypress wood more than a century and a half ago and held its aged head high on the lot that the City of Possumwood kept mowed around it.

Sadly, the derelict structure was wreathed in greedy flames. The first pumper truck arrived, and some former festival goers swarmed it, grabbing gear and hoses. Soon, the fire was hissing angrily at the spray of water. Another truck arrived and added its own stream, drowning the flames into submission.

A teenage girl, curly blonde hair pulled into a messy ponytail, dodged around firefighters and into the smoldering structure. "Sarina! Sarina!" she yelled as she ran.

Whit Bulger dropped his hose and tried to snag her around the waist, but she twisted away from him.

He followed her into the building. "Makayla! Come back!"

Minutes later, he returned, carrying a soggy, unconscious woman over his shoulder.

"Oxygen! And get an ambulance!" He gently set the woman on the ground and charged back inside. She coughed a few times but remained limp on the grass.

He passed Makayla, who was helping a waterlogged girl about her age with a hot pink pixie cut out of the ruins.

Is that Sarina? And her mother? What were they doing in the abandoned cottage?

Whit returned, his beefy arms wrapped around a girl of maybe twelve and a boy a little younger, both dripping wet. They coughed and sputtered but seemed otherwise okay.

As soon as Makayla helped Sarina sit down next to her unconscious mother, she rounded on Whit. "This is all your fault, Daddy!"

"What are you talking about?"

"Sarina's mother had a restraining order against her dad. He was threatening to *kill her*. Sarina, and like the whole family, was *so* happy when he got arrested for robbing that liquor store in Horice. They were finally gonna be safe, at least for a little while. But you— you bonded him out of jail. They had to run away from their own house, Dad. How messed up is that? And before you even ask, yes, I broke into the place. They had to go somewhere."

Whit reached for his daughter's shoulder. "Makayla…"

She dodged out of reach. "Why? Why did you give him the money to get out?"

"It is my job. It's what puts food on the table, Makayla. You want to give up your car? Your fancy cell phone?"

She seethed but said nothing. A siren wailed in the near distance.

Sarina held her mother's head in her lap as one of the firefighters administered oxygen. The other two children sat next to her, bawling. Makayla turned on her heel and plopped on the grass to comfort her friend.

Moments later, EMTs from the Possumwood Volunteer Ambulance Corps pulled up, grabbed their gear, and hurried to where the Sarina's mother lay on the ground. An EMT who PC recognized as Belle Rigel eased the firefighter out of the way and strapped an oxygen mask to the stricken woman's face.

PC spotted Officer Erin Sanchez among the first responders. "Back in a minute, Drew."

Sanchez looked up when PC approached. "Hey, Donovan."

"What a mess, huh?"

The officer shook her head. "That Jeff Stein. What a piece of work."

"Oh, yeah?"

"Our biggest customer. Paula divorced him the first time he got arrested for armed robbery. He didn't take too kindly to that, so she had to get a protective order against him when he got out. I told her she should have moved far away, better yet, to another state. But she said she had roots here. Her kids had friends and their life was finally normal."

"You know her, then?"

"We went to school together. I took the call the last time he beat her. One of her kids called 911. As they were dragging Jeff away, he yelled that she belonged to him, and she'd better not forget it. He'd kill her if she was with another man while he was in jail. Robbed a gas station in Bryan and was out on bail for that. Wouldn't surprise me the least little bit if he found out they were hiding in the cottage and set fire to it out of spite."

"Well, it was lucky most of the fire brigade was just across the street."

"Lucky for the Stein family. Maybe not lucky enough for Dinah Mae Brown."

PC did a double take. "What's she got to do with this?"

"She and the Historical Society were trying to get that old building registered as a historical site. If it gets bulldozed, I guess that opens the way for Thorne Marberger's fancy resort hotel."

"Resort... hotel? I knew he was buying up property, but I hadn't heard about this. I thought he was working with Renetta Sherman to develop a new project on the site of the old Best Southern Motel."

Sanchez shrugged. "No telling with him. He's got plenty of money to do both."

"I don't expect that Caitlyn and Simone will be happy to hear about this."

"Probably not."

Tim Kowalski, who owned the hardware store, walked by, pulling off his tee shirt to blot his sweaty face. Both women stopped talking.

He never misses chest day at the gym. PC shook her head quickly.

"Ned!" he called to a beefy man unbuttoning his turnout coat. "Where's Heidi? Thought she was on call today."

Ned Koehler scuffed his boot on the wet grass and adjusted his ball cap. "She's at her mama's."

"Again?"

Ned nodded.

Kowalski slapped him on the shoulder and they both headed away toward the pumper trucks.

Whit Bulger came out of the house, soot streaking his face. He turned to Sanchez and gestured her over. PC followed.

"Pretty sure it's arson. Let me show you." He stared at the detective.

"It's fine. She works for us." Sanchez reassured him.

They followed Whit into the decimated cottage.

He gestured to a window. "Found a plastic gas can just outside. You see how there's a deep burn in this circle? Goes almost all the way through the floor. Whoever did it must have poured the gas through the window while the family was sleeping near the fireplace, then tossed in a match." Bulger scowled and worked his jaw, as if even the telling of this tale made the words taste foul in his mouth.

PC looked at the charred floor, then across to the stone hearth. A pile of scorched blankets surrounded the fireplace. No. Not just blankets. Quilts. Simone's stolen quilts. She took pictures of them to show to her for confirmation later. Three police cruisers pulled up and their drivers got out. Officers Gorman, Bourgeois, and Fusilier. Someone with Possumwood PD would need to have a chat with Makayla Bulger in the near future.

Sanchez exhaled loudly. "I'll talk to Sarina. See if she saw anything."

The detective trailed along. Paramedics monitored Paula Stein's vitals as she feebly breathed through an oxygen mask. Her eyelids fluttered from time to time, and PC couldn't tell if she was conscious. Sarina stood nearby, an arm around each tear-stained sibling.

The Christmas lighting looky-loos had drifted across the street and become fire scene looky-loos.

Phineas Scott moved to the front of the crowd and clapped his hands. "There's nothing to see here! Time to light the tree. Let's go, people!"

A few people looked over, but everyone else ignored the mayor.

An electronic screech sent the hands of the onlookers flying to cover their ears.

Whit Bulger held a bullhorn to his mouth. "Please clear the area, y'all. You're gonna trample evidence. The mayor wants you back at the park to light up the tree. Y'all best go on over there."

The crowd shifted slightly, but then Gorman, Fusalier, and Bourgeois began herding them away from the burned cottage and they plodded like sluggish cattle to an overgrazed pasture.

PC caught up with Drew.

"What's the scoop?"

"Bulger thinks it's arson."

"Arson?"

"Yes—" PC spotted Caitlyn and Simone Reynolds standing at the corner, across the utility easement. "Come on. I need to talk to them."

Not even the strobes of the fire engines and police cars could compete with the holiday decorations that covered the Afters. A floodlight shone on a life-sized Santa who stood near the chimney with his enormous sack of gifts. A netting of colored lights covered most of the roof, twinkling in a dizzying array of patterns. Lighted icicles drooped from every eave. Evergreen garlands with red bows and gold ornaments wrapped each column on the verandah, and a similar wreath graced the front door.

On the ground, a Mrs. Claus animatronic served a pan of cookies to a group of elves laboring away on a toy assembly line. Santa's sleigh, complete with eight standard and one red-nosed reindeer, sat near the workshop in a lighted drift of cotton sheeting snow. Colored light pooled and danced in the grass, indicating that there were even more decorations around the corner of the house.

PC waved to the women as she and Drew hurried over.

"Caitlyn. Simone." PC nodded to each of them, and Drew raised his hand in greeting.

"What happened, PC?" Simone asked.

"That's what I wanted to talk to you about. Someone set the cottage on fire."

Caitlyn gasped and Simone placed her hand protectively on her wife's back.

PC retrieved her phone. "I have some good news and some bad news."

Simone cocked her head. "Oh?"

"The good news is that I think I found your quilts."

"That's great!" Caitlyn chirped.

PC held out her phone, displaying the ruined blankets. "Now the bad news. They were in the cabin."

"What?" Simone pressed her lips together until they almost disappeared.

"It seems Paula Stein and her three kids were hiding from her abusive ex-husband. They had the quilts."

Caitlyn blinked rapidly.

Simone's hands flew to her hips. "I can't believe Paula Stein would steal from us. If she'd just asked…"

The detective shook her head. "I don't know who stole the quilts. It might have been… someone who was trying to help a friend."

Caitlyn rested her hand just below her throat. "Even if she did take them, it sounds like she had extenuating circumstances." She squeezed her wife's hand. "Don't be so quick to judge."

Simone sighed. "You're probably right. Like usual."

"What are you doing?" Whit Bulger's angry voice shattered the conversation.

He stood at the front corner of the house, talking to someone hidden from view by the building.

"Come back here!"

PC practically ran over to Bulger. "What's going on? Who were you talking to?"

"I have to see Woody." He brushed past her, heading toward the park.

The detective scanned the area, but whoever he'd been talking to had melted into the darkness.

She rejoined Drew and the Reynoldses.

"Who was he yelling at?" Drew asked.

"Didn't see. I want to go find Mama—I don't want her to get done-in by all the excitement. See you ladies later. Sorry about the quilts."

PC and Drew found themselves at the trailing edge of the crowd that had gathered loosely around a twenty-foot evergreen that had been erected in the center front of City Park. The fir was festooned with light strings and gaudy, all-weather ornaments. She caught sight of Terry's nearly audible red jacket and she wormed her way through the throng of distracted people. Throwing the switch to turn on the Christmas tree lights couldn't compare to the excitement of watching a house burn down.

Rose stretched her arm high in the air and waved as soon as she spotted PC and Drew.

Mayor Scott's lackluster voice limped from the PA system. "… and now, let there be lights."

For a few seconds, nothing happened. Then the tree glowed with red, green, blue, and yellow lights. Random claps and half-hearted cheers greeted the spectacle.

Shame. It really is a pretty tree. "Mama? Terry? You ready to go home?"

"I'm ready, honey. But I need to stop by the Baptist Church real quick. I think I left my scarf in the choir loft on Thursday."

PC raised an eyebrow. "Is anyone going to be there this time of night?"

"Sure," Terry replied. "Bart Hornsby'll be there another twenty minutes or so."

The detective turned to Drew. "Need a lift?"

He winked at her. "I can probably make it across the street. But thanks. I'll call you tomorrow."

"Sounds good."

He squeezed her shoulder and headed toward his house. Her car was somewhere in the mirror-image lot on the opposite side of the park.

Rose turned her head toward the Afters. "That's a real shame about that cottage catchin' on fire and all. What happened, honey?"

"Not sure yet, Mama."

Terry put his arm around PC's mother. "Rose, my darling dear, you should know better than to ask your daughter about on-going cases."

The parking lot lights had been turned off so the town Christmas tree could take center stage, and the detective had to find her car in the dark by pressing the unlock button until the vehicle chirped and the interior lights came on. Once everyone was loaded inside, she drove the short distance to the *Justice Avenue Baptist Church*. They made their way from the parking lot to the grand front entrance.

"I'll just be a minute." Rose disappeared into the lobby.

Moments later, an eardrum-rending scream echoed off the imported Italian marble tiles.

Chapter 4

"MAMA!" PC SPRINTED into the *Justice Avenue Baptist Church's* sanctuary, Terry not far behind.

Rose stood near the pulpit with her hands on her face. Terry ran over and threw his arms around her. PC faced the darkened choir loft.

Whit Bulger lay face-up on the crimson carpet, his neck at an awkward angle.

The wooden safety railing along the edge of the choir loft hung in two jagged pieces.

"He must have fallen." Terry kept his arms around Rose, preventing her from turning to see the body again.

"So it would seem. Why don't you get her out of here, and I'll call the PD."

Terry nodded and led Rose out into the lobby.

PC knelt and checked for a pulse but detected nothing. She pulled out her phone, studying the body. She'd seen many a jumper in her twenty-five-year homicide career. Something wasn't right here. Whether the fall was accidental or intentional, he would have been really unlucky to die from the ten-foot drop from the choir loft. For most people, that's a survivable height, likely with only minor injuries, if any.

"9-1-1. What's your emergency?"

"Annie?"

"PC?"

"There's been… an incident. It looks like Whit Bulger fell out of the choir loft at the Baptist church."

"I'll get EMS on the way."

"No. Send Dr. Mack."

"Dr. Mack? He's the Medical Examiner, not a—" Silence. "Oh."

"Thanks, Annie."

PC hung up.

She regarded the corpse. *I thought you were going to see Woody. Why are you here, on the opposite side of town?*

Hoping to get some clues from the architectural layout, PC studied the stadium-style sanctuary. Two aisles divided the congregation into three sections. A balcony at the back of the church offered additional seating. At the front of the church, altar rails with cushions at their bases for people to kneel on divided the laity from the clergy. Gaps in the barrier, in line with the aisleways, included a small step up, as the chancel was raised. A few feet behind the railing, were two pulpits, one on either side of the sanctuary. The organist had an alcove behind the left lectern. At the back of the chancel was another raised section. This is where the performers sang, danced, and acted on Tuesday nights.

An ornately carved wooden altar, draped with a purple cloth, loomed in front of a lap pool-sized baptismal font that was raised off the stage a few feet, with steps at either end. Did they perform a swim-through ceremony? A stained-glass window was positioned so it would color the water when the sun shone through it. Above that was the choir loft with the broken railing.

The detective trotted up the stairs. Hymnals strewn on the floor of the loft were the only evidence that anything was amiss. Had Bulger struggled with someone? Perhaps the person he'd argued with at the cottage? PC regretted that she hadn't caught sight of him. Or her.

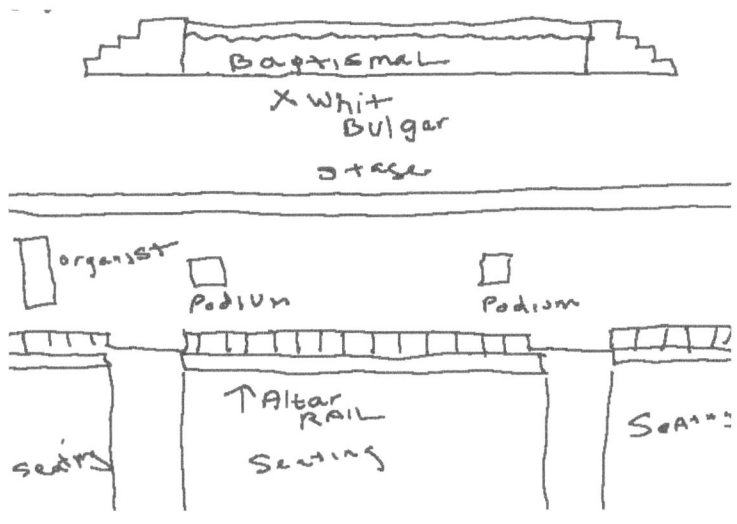

Voices came from the lobby. Males. Had the PD arrived? She moved to the edge of the loft. Woody, accompanied by Tran and Gorman, walked into the sanctuary. The chief was gaunt and haggard.

PC's heart sank as he and his escorts made their way to the front of the church. Woody's eyes caught hers, and his eyebrows rose.

He shook his head. "Donovan. Should have known. You're the Typhoid Mary of murder."

"How are you feeling, Woody?"

"I've been better."

Tran surveyed the still form on the floor before he looked up at PC. "What happened?"

"Mama forgot her scarf, came back to get it, and found him."

Woody tapped Gorman on the shoulder. "Go get her statement."

Tran snapped some photos. "Looks like he broke his neck in the fall."

PC shrugged. "That's how it appears."

The chief's eyes narrowed. "You don't think that's what happened?"

"A ten-foot fall might kill my mama. But Whit Bulger? He's a big ole boy. Very fit. Very strong. And onto thickly padded carpet, no less. Might have an easier time believing that if not for the argument"

Woody steadied himself on the pulpit. "What argument?"

"At the scene of the fire. He had words with someone, but I couldn't see who. He said he was on his way to see you."

The chief frowned. "He never showed up at the station."

Tran looked from Woody to PC. "Jeff Stein jumped bail. Whit wasn't just a bail bondsman and process server. He was also a fugitive recovery agent. What if he saw Stein duck into the church?"

Woody picked up the thread. "Stein tried to hide in the choir loft, they struggled, and Whit lost. It could have happened that way. He's already got a warrant, so we need to flush him out and bring him in."

PC crossed her arms. "I agree Stein should be interviewed. And not just about Bulger, here. Good chance he knows something about that fire at the cottage his family was hiding in."

"Miss Rose didn't have much of a statement." Gorman's voice came from a doorway to the lobby, and PC wondered how long he'd been standing in the shadows.

"Where are they, Bart?" Dr. Mack's voice boomed from the lobby.

A sixty-ish man appeared in the doorway near Gorman.

That must be Bart Hornsby.

Dr. Mack squeezed past him and hurried down the aisle. He gazed at Whit Bulger for a moment before setting down his fishing tackle box of equipment and pulling on some nitrile gloves. Gorman squirmed when the doctor took Bulger's temperature.

The ME wrote something in a notebook. "He hasn't even started to cool off yet. Time of death was within the last half hour."

Mama must have just missed the fall. Or the murder. A shudder ran down PC's body. "I saw him about twenty minutes ago at the cottage fire. He must have come straight here and…"

The doctor tucked his notebook into his tackle box, then took a photo of the body. "Tran, would you be good enough to help me roll him over?"

"Sure."

Nothing seemed to be out of the ordinary. No bruises, abrasions, or wounds. But bruises took a while to color up and could be affected by postmortem lividity.

"Maybe he *did* die from the fall," PC said.

"Wonder why his shirt is damp?" Dr. Mack scanned the empty floor around the body.

PC looked at Bulger. "He was pretty sweaty from all the fire gear when I saw him earlier." *Must have taken a moment to wash his sooty face. And who wouldn't?*

Dr. Mack nodded. "I can believe that."

Tran took a few more photos of the body.

Low voices drew PC's attention. Two men from Clay's Funeral Home wheeled a gurney with a neatly folded cadaver pouch on it down the aisle.

"Well," PC looked at Woody. "I guess you guys will be here a while. I need to get Mama back home."

"Night, Donovan."

Tran nodded. "Talk to you in the morning."

"Later." PC hotfooted it to Rose and Terry, waiting in the lobby.

Terry's face was drawn. "We've got to get her home."

Rose was pale and shaking.

"Mama, I'm so sorry you had to see that. Let's get you back to the house. I'll make you some of that relaxing tea I bought earlier."

PC handed Terry her keys. Go get Mama in the car. I'll be right behind you."

She watched them exit the lobby before she turned to the sexton standing by the entrance to the sanctuary. "Mr. Hornsby? Did you hear anything?"

He shook his head. "No, not a thing. I was in the back office, getting ready to lock up."

"Is the church usually open in the evenings?"

Hornsby nodded. "The sanctuary is open for anyone who wants to come in to pray, but there's no access to any other part of the church."

"Thanks, Mr. Hornsby." The detective hurried to her car.

PC sat on the bed, legs crossed. Cordite snuggled behind her. In front lay a burgundy three-ring binder. Her father's murder book. Woody had given her a copy when she first arrived back in Possumwood, although, for some time, she hadn't known he was the one who'd left it in her car. Her hands rested on the closed cover as she tried to corral the runaway thoughts careening through her brain.

Whit Bulger's death didn't make sense to her. It was possible he fell, or was pushed, out of the choir loft. Ten feet was high enough to break his neck if he landed on his head. A head that was clean shaven. Any bruising or rug burn would have been easy to spot, but there was nothing. She was missing something, she knew that.

While the fresh crime scene percolated in the back of her mind, she looked through the cold one in the binder. Perhaps this time something would come to her on this case. What had she found out?

A Colt Python .357 was found buried under a driveway that had been poured in the same general time frame as her father's murder. Ballistics comparison between it and the recovered casing and slug from the deadly ShopStop robbery was inconclusive.

Her friend from NASA had enhanced a window reflection for her. It was not very clear but could have been the image of someone wearing a rodeo trophy belt buckle. Half the people in Mirabella County had at least one of those.

Her father had acquired an elaborate black and white mosaic box on a business trip to the Middle East. He'd used it to collect donations to a children's hospital charity at the cash register. The killer had taken it away with him. Had he kept it as a trophy, or was it rotting in a landfill?

The prevailing theory at the time of Trey Donovan's murder was that someone passing through town robbed the ShopStop and shot him in the process. However, if the driveway gun was the same one used in the crime, that would indicate someone local. How would an out-of-towner know about a subdivision under construction off the beaten path? Seemed like an awfully big coincidence, but she couldn't prove it was the murder weapon.

Her finger traced the image of her father's body sprawled face down over the counter. Why didn't he duck down behind it? He had a gun there. He could have crawled to the office and locked himself in if he was being threatened. Instead, he stood there, perhaps talking to the robber.

Like it was someone he knew.

Nausea roiled her stomach. Was there someone here in Possumwood keeping a terrible, forty-year-old secret? Someone who passed her on the street and said hello, knowing full well how much they'd wrecked her life, but pretending nothing had happened?

"What?" Terry shouted from the living room.

PC jumped up to see what was wrong.

He was on his feet in front of the couch, his phone to his ear. "How are they not canceling the cantata?… I know… I guess that's true. It *would* be great tribute to all the hard work Whit put into it. Well, Reverend Costas has been angling to direct the thing since the beginning…. No… Yeah, I'll tell her."

"Who was that?" Rose asked.

PC was behind them, so she stayed quiet and listened.

"Winnie Hargraves. She said that Richard Costas is going to take Whit Bulger's place as choir director for the cantata."

The detective could hear the eye-roll in her mother's voice. "I can't believe they still wanna have it." She shook her head.

"Winnie pointed out that Whit worked so hard organizing, it would be such a shame to let all of that effort go to waste. We should honor him by going on with it."

"Guess I can see that. It's just…" She chewed her lip. "Richard is workin' hard to rebuild the Justice Avenue Baptist Church, but that don't explain why he was so desperate to be the director. Guess he got his wish."

PC tapped her upper lip. *Desperate, huh? Desperate enough to kill for it?*

Chapter 5

PC CREPT BACK to her bedroom, hoping that neither Terry nor Rose noticed she'd been eavesdropping on their conversation. Reverend Costas seemed so eager to direct the choir that he was happy to snatch the baton from Whit Bulger's still-cooling fingers, but did he give him a little nudge over the choir loft railing?

The detective got into bed but couldn't find a comfortable position. Questions about Whit Bulger, and the realization that her father might have known his killer, agitated her brain like a washing machine with an unbalanced load. Experience told her that stress often produced her recurring nightmare. It always started out as an ordinary trip to the grocery store. Only each shopper or employee was one of the bloodied victims of cases she'd investigated. Best not to sleep at this point.

"Wanna go for a walk, Cordie?"

The dog's ears pricked up and he raised his head.

PC dressed and slipped on a jacket. With any luck, the fresh night air would clear her busy brain and allow her to quiet her mind. She grabbed her keys and his leash, and they set out for a stroll. The waxing gibbous moon, only a few days off full, cast a silvery half-light over the sleeping neighborhood. Even though November had waned, and December was stretching her wings, most trees were still fully clothed in late summer leaves. Truman Parker's prize-winning roses bloomed in delight from the cooler, wetter weather. Fall was fickle on the coastal plain—one day it might be 90°, the next could be in the 40s. Tonight, it felt like low 50s, and PC zipped her light jacket the rest of the way.

Woody was right. Jeff Stein was the most likely suspect in the Bulger case. He was a violent felon who'd threatened to kill his own family and didn't think twice about violating a protective order. Was he also the firebug who set the cottage they were hiding from him in ablaze? And this clearly wasn't his first prison rodeo.

And even if that was true, District Attorney Travis Bailey couldn't convict Stein for Bulger's death just because he nearly murdered his own family and Bulger stopped it. Right now, the homicide 'evidence' amounted to nothing more than speculation.

If Bulger was in the process of tracking down Stein for skipping bail, surely City Bail Bonds had records of his investigation. Did he call the office before he ran into the church after Stein?

If that's what happened.

And why was he over there, anyway? He was going to see Woody, on the other side of town. That seems off, too. If he set eyes on Stein, why didn't he just apprehend him? That was his job when he had his bounty hunter hat on.

Maybe it wasn't Stein he'd been shouting at.

Cordite stopped, his ears turned toward some bushes. Branches shuddered as something large crashed around in the shrubbery. The dog gave a low growl. PC couldn't see what was causing the movement, and that was worse than the noise the hidden thing was making. She started backing away, visions of rabid coyotes or aggressive raccoons dancing in her head.

The terrier stayed rooted to the ground, the leash growing taut.

"Cordite! Hurry up! Come on, let's go!"

He leaned into the harness, his hackles rising.

Branches parted, and a dark form shuffled into the open.

The agitated dog barked.

The startled armadillo jumped straight up, nearly a foot in the air, and scurried back into the plants.

The relieved detective laughed.

"Thanks for saving me from dangerous wild animals." She tugged on the leash.

Cordite was desperate to sniff where the armadillo had been, so she let him. That little shot of adrenalin was enough to break her mind out of the stress loop she'd been caught in.

PC yawned. "Come on, Cordie. Let's go home."

The alarm was a nagging harpy that rousted PC out of bed almost as soon as she had settled into a deep sleep. But she couldn't hit snooze. Rose's rescue critters expected their meals to be delivered on time, so she made her way out to the barn to scoop grain and throw hay.

Guinevere, the beige donkey, flicked a radar dish ear towards PC as the detective scratched her shoulder. Arthur, the black donkey, was still nibbling his hay. Three-legged Hazel looked on, as if the goat hoped an extra cookie might fall out of PC's pocket at any time. After a few minutes, she gave up and wandered to the water trough.

Arthur finished his breakfast and sauntered over to PC and Gwen. Because his blind side was closest to the detective, she was careful to talk to him, so he didn't startle as she reached to scratch along the top of his scraggly mane. He flinched at her touch, but not enough for Guinevere to switch into guardian mode.

"Alright, I can't stand here and scratch you two all day."

PC unlatched the gate and undid the snap that held the chain around the post. Guinevere was fond of adventuring, and her favorite conquest was Truman Parker's rose bushes. She'd made good her escape a few times, until a simple double-ended snap and a chain had put an end to her escapologist endeavors.

PC headed to the house and found Chirp, one of the semi-feral cats that inhabited Rose's back porch, sitting in front of an empty food dish, the cat's large orange eyes glaring malevolently at her.

The detective eased past the cantankerous calico and opened the cabinet that held the food. Once she'd topped off the dish with kibble, she was allowed passage into the house. Cordite usually escorted her out to feed, but his late-night walkies apparently dampened his morning outdoor urgency. Just as well. Even though she was the smallest of the four, the fierce cats were his arch enemies. But they never seemed to tussle with Blossom, the opossum who lived under the porch.

Rose sat at the breakfast table, drinking a cup of coffee and picking at a slice of buttered toast. "You know, honey, I sure have a taste for Winnie Hargraves' eggs benedict. You wanna go to the City Café?"

"Let me wash my hands first, Mama." The prospect of a hot breakfast that she didn't have to clean up after was very appealing, given her sleep-deprived state.

PC dried her hands. "I'm ready whenever you are."

"Lemme call Terry and see if he wants to go."

"I'll take Cordie out the front for a minute."

When she returned, Rose had gathered her purse and phone and was waiting by the front door.

PC unleashed Cordite and shook her head. She'd have to wash her hands again when they got to the restaurant. "What did Terry say?"

"He'll meet us on the sidewalk in front of his house. Says he's got some news."

"About what?"

"Didn't say."

By the time PC got the car pulled out of the driveway, Terry was halfway there. Living two doors down from one's significant other had its advantages. In a canary yellow waistcoat, he was impossible to miss—he had the most colorful, and some would go as far as gaudy—wardrobe of anyone PC knew, Possumwood or Houston, and all points in between.

Shaking his head, he climbed into the back seat of PC's SUV next to Rose. "I can't believe it."

Rose gave him a peck on the cheek. "What can't you believe?"

"The artifacts!"

PC frowned in the rear-view mirror. "What artifacts?"

"At the cottage! They came to look at it in the daylight. You know, to see if there was any additional evidence? But they found some old jewelry and silverware. Not sure what else. Like it had fallen out of the walls or something. Years ago, Dinah Mae had everything in that little cottage packed up and put on display at the Quenton Plantation, so these must have been hidden somewhere. The second she gets word, anything they might even think of doing to that house will come to a full halt."

PC pulled up at a stop sign. "There's a lot of stonework in that cottage. May not even need demolition."

"I hope so! We do not need Thorne Marberger's resort hotel in town right next to the Afters. Probably don't need it at all, truth be told. That'd butt right up against Drew's back yard. Bet he don't want it, either," Rose said.

PC waited to turn left onto Main. "Who actually owns this property? Aside from the storefronts on the north end and Drew's house, it's a vacant lot. And of course, the cottage in the southeast corner."

"That's a good question." Terry replied. "It's my understanding that the county owns it. They pay the city to mow it, but Thorne Marberger is trying to make some claim that it should never have been seized for delinquent taxes and it rightfully belongs to his family. He has enough money to pay double or triple what the land's worth, so Mirabella County might rather take his money than fight about it in court. The only hitch in that get-along was that Dinah Mae Brown has been trying to get it declared as a state historic site—the Afters already is. If that happens, it's no use to Marberger—he has to tear down the cottage to put up his fancy hotel."

So at least two people have motive to set the cottage on fire—Stein and Marberger. Interesting.

"How are the Reynoldses able to live at the Afters and use it as a business, then?" PC pulled the car into a parking slot at the back of the *City Café*.

Rose unbuckled. "There's nothin' says you can't live in a designated historic site. It's just you gotta get approval from the Historic people for everything you do—paintin', landscapin', all that stuff."

PC pulled open the door and stopped.

The room was full of agitated people, and PC recognized most of them.

Jim Hargraves stood on a chair. "I would rather see the *entire* town of Possumwood burn before that happens!"

Chapter 6

RENETTA SHERMAN, POSSUMWOOD's real estate lady, jerked herself to her feet. "That resort will destroy the town! Mark my words. If we're gonna go, we should go on our own terms, fighting for our lives."

PC leaned toward Rose. "Looks like now's not a good time."

"Y'all come on in," Winnie Hargraves called from behind the cash register.

"Don't you think you're bein' a bit dramatic there, Jim? You, too, Renetta?" Justice Johnson, Rose's closest friend, asked.

Renetta's eyes blazed. "Do you remember what happened over in Angleberry when that monster discount store opened up? Almost all the mom-and-pop businesses closed." Her glare turned to Winnie. "And don't think just because you have a restaurant, you'll be safe. Thorne's plannin' on havin' at least three restaurants onsite."

Guess Renetta is a bit miffed about Thorne's plan to go into direct competition with her boutique hotel project.

PC, Rose, and Terry slunk to Justice's table near the back of the restaurant.

"I'm going to wash my hands," PC whispered to Rose.

She tiptoed to the restrooms, listening to Renetta's rant instead of paying attention to where she was going. She caught her shoe on the corner of a large box against the wall and nearly went sprawling.

The picture on the cardboard was of an artificial Christmas tree, twinkling with red, blue, and green lights. Just like the one Rose had. In an instant, PC was a child again. Mama was making hot cocoa in the kitchen and Daddy was trying not to swear as he untangled the strings of lights that had been wantonly tossed into the box last year. Daisy and Rocky argued about who got to put up the first ornament.

Rocky said it should be him because he was the littlest.

Daisy said it should be her because she was the middle kid and was never, ever first for anything, if they went by birthdays.

PC focused on stringing popcorn and cranberry garlands to put out for the birds.

The ladies' room door opened, breaking the reverie. A woman squeezed past the detective in the narrow hallway. PC walked in in to wash her hands. Perhaps when they got back from breakfast, Rocky'd be awake and they could put up the tree.

As PC re-entered the dining room, a man raised a cup of coffee. He was one of the pastors from the disastrous cantata preview yesterday. *What was his name? He was in charge of refreshments. Steve Anders.*

"Surely, these new artifacts will at least delay any demolition. If the stonework hasn't been damaged too badly, the cottage might be restorable. When I spoke to Dinah Mae—"

"You spoke with her already?" asked Truman Parker.

"Yes. I was on one of the pumper trucks yesterday. Still there with Chief Lopez when the Department of Public Safety arson investigators showed up. It was late, maybe 10:00. They found a few objects that looked very old spilling out of the damaged walls inside the structure. You all know I'm a member of the Mirabella County Historical Society, so, of course I'd call the president."

"Isn't gettin' Dinah Mae involved impedin' the arson investigation?" Parker shot back.

Anders snorted. "Chief didn't need to call DPS. There was a strong smell of gasoline inside. Couldn't be anything but arson—don't need the state police to tell us that."

Frida, the server, arrived at their table, order pad in hand. "Eggs Benedict, Miz Donovan?"

Rose grinned. "You got my number, honey."

The rest of the table made their own orders, and Frida left for the kitchen.

PC looked around the dining room. Now that the demolition was forestalled, the tension over Thorne Marberger's theoretical resort gradually dissipated, and folks got back to their breakfasting. Steve Anders picked up his check and started toward the cash register, passing by PC's table.

Justice shook her head. "Poor ole Whit Bulger. Such a shame."

"Is it?" Anders muttered as he passed.

"I'm sorry. What did you say?" PC was shocked to hear someone, a man of the cloth no less, speaking ill of the dead in public.

Anders paused and nodded to Rose and Terry. "Ms. Donovan. Mr. Gillespie." His eyes rolled over Justice like he thought she might bite him before they fell on PC. "I don't believe we've met."

Rose smiled. "This is my daughter, Primrose. She's been here helpin' me out since I had my fall."

"You're getting around so well, I'd forgotten you'd broken your hip." The minister regarded PC. "It's not a secret that Whit Bulger and I... did not see eye to eye. I hope that God's Grace surrounds his family in their time of sorrow, but I am an imperfect man, and as much as I have prayed about Mr. Bulger's decisions, I have not yet found the strength to forgive him. As I tell my congregation, forgiveness is a process. It was a pleasure meeting you, but I have an appointment, and I need to go."

The detective turned to Rose, who cast her eyes to the table.

Justice stirred creamer into her coffee. "It was his brother. Alvin wasn't a bad fella, 'less he was liquored up. Kinda a ne'er to well, though. Seems he had an allergy to gainful employment. So when that bartender, used to be at the Silver Dollar—he quit after that—he cut Alvin off, cuz he was drunker'n a skunk. Alvin hit him with a chair and broke his shoulder. The po-lice came to pick 'im up. Alvin tried bailin' himself out of the pokey, but Whit wouldn't give him a bond. He didn't have no job and nothin' of value for collateral. Steve and his wife were out of town at some big church conference and didn't get back until a week later. So he couldn't sign for Alvin."

She sipped her coffee.

"Aren't there two bail bonds shops in Possumwood? What's the one by the courthouse?"

"Justice Bail Bonds. But Merlo Abrams wasn't gonna take a chance on him, neither. Anyway, while Alvin was coolin' his heels, he got on the wrong side of some 200 pounds of trouble callin' itself Oscar Fry. Poor ole Alvin never had a chance."

PC picked up her own coffee mug. "He got beaten up?"

Terry patted Rose's hand.

Justice raised an eyebrow. "Oh, you could say that. Whit felt real bad about it and sent flowers to the funeral, but Steve had a hissy fit and tossed 'em out on the curb."

Move over, Jeff Stein. You've got some company on the suspect list. "Did you notice any conflict between the reverend and the… Mr. Bulger, Mama?"

Rose dabbed at her lips with a napkin. "Well, of course there was gonna be some tension, honey. But Reverend Anders didn't really come to rehearsals—there was no need. He wasn't singin'."

Frida arrived at their table and began distributing plates. She set a small glass bowl of jam next to Terry. "Here's your special preserves, Mr. G."

He grinned. "Thanks, Frida."

PC recalled that he was quite the foodie, always experimenting with recipes and cooking techniques, but it seemed a little presumptuous that he'd have a stock of 'special preserves' at a restaurant. She let it go and focused on her meal. Her omelet came with a side of avocado toast and the roasted garlic mixed with the smashed avocado was so good PC almost forgot about the eggs.

Martha Henry, the Methodist pastor, burst into the café, arms full of fliers and a roll of masking tape around her wrist like a bracelet.

"Winnie!" she called.

"What've you got there, Martha?"

The reverend grinned. "I was talking with Simone Reynolds yesterday evening. She told me about some of their quilts being stolen off the clothesline, then turning up in the fire. I thought we could rally the quilters in the community to replace them. If we make extras, we could give them to the less fortunate who come to the church in need of assistance."

"I think that's a real good idea, Martha. But you might wanna wait 'til after Christmas. Folks who make their own gifts are probably a mite busy just now."

Martha's shoulders drooped. "I hadn't thought about that. Can I still put up a flier? I could write, 'Resolve to quilt in January' or something on there."

Terry watched the Reverend pull out a marker and write on a flier. "She's got a million ideas, doesn't she?"

Rose nodded as she chewed. "You're smirkin' but she did come up with some good ones for the cantata. I wish Whit hadn't got so put out with her for sharin' 'em."

PC's forkful of egg halted halfway to her mouth. "Oh?"

Justice stood up and fished in her jeans pocket for her wallet. "Before y'all get to gossipin' about the cantata, I'm gonna go to the hardware store and pick up that lye Tim ordered for me before I get too far behind on my soap makin.'"

"I need to get some more bar soap from you—I'm almost out," Terry said as she laid some bills on the table. "Tut! Tut! Keep your money." He handed the cash back to her.

"Thank you kindly for breakfast. I'll be at the farmers' market Saturday, in my usual spot. I'll make sure to have a couple bars set aside for you. Folks really like that goatmilk soap. Sells out quick, 'specially this time of year, with all the holiday shoppin.'"

PC chewed her eggs as Justice walked away. The detective swallowed and turned to her mother. "Mama, what were you gonna say about Martha and Whit?"

Rose picked at a piece of English muffin with her fork. "Lydia quit drivin' a while ago, so whenever she was gonna play the organ somewhere, Martha drove her, whether she was preachin' or not. Martha sat through the rehearsals in the congregation seatin'. Now, Whit put the shortest singers in the front and the tallest in the back, with the different parts kinda willy-nilly. Martha said she thought it would sound better if they were grouped by voice, like the baritones together, and the tenors next to them, and so on. No idea why he got so heated over her suggestion. She was in the audience, listenin', after all."

Terry chuckled. "May have sounded better, but I expect we have some singers that probably shouldn't be next to each other."

Rose pursed her lips. "Be that as it may, he coulda been more cordial about it. She was just tryin' to help."

"You know how he is. Doesn't think women belong in the clergy. Wouldn't be the first clash they've had." Terry pushed his empty plate away.

The cowbell on the front door jingled. Tran and Gorman walked in. The younger officer smiled and gave her a little wave, but Gorman acted like he didn't see her. They sat at the counter and Frida brought them coffee.

Terry raised his hand to get her attention and mimed writing on his hand. She nodded and came over with the check. They stood, and PC reached for her bag.

"No, no. My treat." Terry grinned.

"We didn't invite you so you could pay," PC replied.

"Please do not deprive me of the pleasure of purchasing a meal for three beautiful ladies."

"Well... Thank you for breakfast, then."

As Terry headed to the register, PC saw that Tran was now alone. She approached his stool, and he spun around to greet her.

"Hey, PC."

"Tran. Barely had a chance to catch up since you've been back. Sounds like you had a great honeymoon, even if you did study instead of enjoying yourself."

He gave her a sly smile. "Oh, we did plenty of that, don't worry."

The officer poured some creamer into his coffee and began stirring. His phone chimed. "Hold on a sec."

Tran's spoon clattered to his saucer. "Chief thinks they've found Jeff Stein, and he may be barricaded."

Chapter 7

TRAN GLANCED OVER his shoulder, toward the front door. "Look, PC. I know this is a big ask, since you're not on the payroll on this one, but I would feel a lot better if you came along."

She hesitated. "I don't want to just abandon my mom at the City Café. If Stein is barricaded, it could take a while."

Tran looked at the table where Rose sat with Terry and Justice. "It's a huge imposition, but…"

PC rolled her bottom lip between her teeth. "Let me see if Terry'll take her home."

She strode over to the table. "Tran needs my help with something. Terry, if I give you my keys, are you okay to drive Mama back to the house?"

"Sure. Good luck."

"We may need it."

Tran's cruiser rolled to a stop in front of the St. Lucia Catholic Church. Three other squads, including Gorman's, were already there. According to the limestone-encased sign, early mass should be over soon.

PC frowned. "So how reliable is this info?"

Tran shrugged. "Not sure. All I know is as soon as we got to the City Café, Gorman got a call and stepped outside. Few minutes later, he texts me and says a tip came in that Stein's holed up in the Catholic church."

"Does he have the warrants? If the priest is harboring Stein, he'll want to see it."

Tran rubbed his eyes and reached for the door handle. "Don't think so. He can show him the warrants on the computer, though."

PC unfolded her legs and stood, looking around the full parking lot. "Woody coming to this shindig?"

Tran shook his head. "No. He's staying close to his office today."

She sighed. He'd been having more and more bad days. *People on chemo get worse before they get better, right?* PC shivered, the chill from her insides spilling out. "Then I guess we'd better do him proud."

"Tran! Get your butt over here!" Gorman shouted from the sidewalk.

He and PC headed toward the other officers.

Gorman scowled at PC. "Why are you here? Just because you and the Chief go way back, he throws you a bone now and again, but don't expect that when—" He stopped himself abruptly.

He's gone and you're chief? Anger flickered across her heart, and her words came out clipped and harsher than she'd intended. "I'll bear that in mind. Officer. Gorman."

Gorman turned away from her and started up the walk to the ornately carved wooden doors of the sanctuary.

PC quickened her pace to catch up with him. "We're waiting until mass lets out before we go in there, right?"

"Why? We know where Stein is, and the priest's not going to lie before his whole congregation, now is he?"

The detective resisted the urge to grab Gorman by the ear. "Look, if you barge in and confront Father Benavides in front of his flock, he's not going to cooperate. He's gonna need to prove that he will protect them, no matter what. Just wait until he's done and speak with him in private."

Gorman's eyes narrowed. "We do stuff different out here than in the big city. In fact, maybe when you go back to Houston, you can call up your old buddies and get Tran a job there."

"But I'm not—"

"I don't care." Gorman pushed past her.

Tran elbowed PC. "You're not what? Going back to Houston?"

Before she could answer, Gorman threw open the doors to the church.

Father Benavides stopped in mid-benediction.

"Where is he?" Gorman demanded.

The parishioners murmured among themselves.

"I'm afraid I have no idea what you're talking about. Please. Allow me to finish this morning's mass, and I'll be happy to discuss whatever this is with you afterward."

Gorman continued up the aisle toward the altar. "We'll discuss this now. I know you're hiding him."

"Hiding who?" Father Benavides took a step back as Gorman violated his personal space.

"Don't play innocent with me. Turn him over."

The muttering of the congregation grew louder.

PC turned to Tran, her eyes flicking across the churchgoers. "We need to get them out of here."

He nodded and put the other two officers on crowd control duty.

The snick of metal on metal made PC's head whip back around toward the front of the church, only to see Gorman handcuffing Father Benavides.

Appalled, she rushed over. "What are you doing? You can't handcuff the priest in the middle of mass."

"I can and I have. Now he's going to tell me what I want to know."

"Stop this nonsense, Gorman! Uncuff him and show him the warrants. I'm sure he'll understand if he knows what's going on."

Gorman glared at her. "I have probable cause—someone reported that Jeff Stein was here in the church, asking for asylum."

Asylum? This isn't an embassy.

Father Benavides craned his head over his shoulder. "Jeff Stein? He isn't here. And if he were, I'd counsel him to turn himself in to the authorities."

"Of course, you'd say that."

Tran used his own handcuff key to release the priest.

"Hey!" Gorman protested.

Benavides rubbed the red marks on his wrists. "Thank you."

"You're welcome, Father." Tran's jaw clenched and he turned on Gorman. "Where did you get this hot tip?"

"A very reliable source."

"Who?"

Gorman's lips tightened. "Fine. My brother-in-law called me to say that his cousin told him that he overheard someone in Marberger's grocery store saying that Stein was hiding out here. And my brother-in-law is honest as the day is long."

PC's mouth gaped open like a broken door. "*That's* your probable cause?"

Tran turned toward the priest. "Father Benavides, on behalf of the Possumwood Police Department, I want to offer my sincerest apologies for this unfortunate misunderstanding. Officer Gorman is very eager to capture Whit Bulger's killer, and he overstepped his bounds."

A wan smile traced its way across the priest's lips. "I understand his misplaced enthusiasm. We all want to find the person responsible for this terrible tragedy and bring justice for Mr. Bulger's family. He was a beloved member of our church."

"Thank you, Father."

PC and Tran hustled Gorman out of the sanctuary and into the parking lot, where the parishioners milled about, rubbernecking as the doors opened.

"We're going to the chief," Tran hissed at Gorman.

The older officer's nostrils flared, but he got into his car and started it up.

Tran slammed his door after he got in the car. "What was he thinking? He knows better than that. Any other place, this would be a major lawsuit. Still might."

PC lurched against her seatbelt as Tran slammed on the brakes. Two pedestrians were so deep in conversation they failed to notice the police cruiser when they stepped into the street.

She readjusted the shoulder strap. "He did seem somewhat forgiving, given that Bulger was a member of his church. But you're right. Gorman was way over the line. Like several miles over."

Tran used the hands free to call Woody and tell him what happened while they drove to the Possumwood Police Station. When they arrived, Gorman was already in Woody's office. Tran and PC slipped in quietly and stood at the back.

"… I got carried away. I'm sorry."

Woody leaned forward in his chair. "You got carried away? Really? This ain't the kind of job where you can allow yourself to get carried away."

"Well, sir, you told me to check it out and to take Tran with me. That's what I did."

A little color flushed Woody's pallid cheeks. "You tried to brute force a priest to turn in a fugitive who wasn't even at the church. I hate to think of what would have happened if Tran and Donovan hadn't been there. Were you going to get out the rubber hose and beat a confession out of Father Benavides while you were there?"

Gorman hung his head. "No, sir."

"Hand 'em over."

"What?"

"Your badge and your gun. Hand 'em over. You're on administrative leave until further notice."

"But Chief!"

"You're lucky you still have a job."

Gorman rose and placed the requested items on Woody's desk, then turned on his heel. Sparing a baleful glare at PC and Tran, he stormed out of the chief's office.

Woody slumped against the back of his chair. "That went well."

Tran glanced over his shoulder. "Father Benavides seemed to be very understanding."

The chief leaned his forehead against his hand, the armrest squeaking under his elbow. "I sure hope so. I'll give him a call and make sure we're copacetic."

Woody picked up the handset on his desk phone. PC followed Tran to his cube.

He opened his laptop. "Give me a minute to check on a few things, then I'll run you back home."

"Sure. Want some coffee?"

"That'd be great. Black is fine."

The detective walked to the miniscule break room and got the bean brew. She returned to find Tran frowning over his screen.

"Well, looks like we've found Jeff Stein after all."

Chapter 8

"WHERE IS HE?" PC blurted.

Tran let out a loud, protracted breath. "Stein's been in the drunk tank in Tulsa since around 2 AM Saturday. They were about to cut him loose when they noticed he had felony warrants. They're holding him for us."

PC nodded slowly. "So, Stein has motive, and probably means, but zero opportunity."

"That about sums it up. Guess we should tell the chief."

PC followed him down the hall, where he stuck his head in the door and gave the news to his boss.

The chief frowned.

Tran shifted his weight. "Should we send Bourgeois and Fusilier to pick him up?"

Woody shook his head. "Since he jumped bail on the armed robbery charge in Horice, I'm going to refer it to the Sheriff's Office. He obviously didn't kill Whit Bulger. Even if he did, he'd end up in County, anyway. He's their problem now."

"I'll call Sid's office." Tran fished his phone out of his pocket as he headed back toward his cube.

PC waited for Tran to finish his phone call. Sidney Justice occasionally played darts on Wednesday nights at the Biersal when PC and her friends were there. He had been two years ahead of her in school, and all those years ago, he was the last person she'd have expected to be the Mirabella County Sheriff.

She thought she remembered Rose saying he was Santa at the tree lighting ceremony yesterday, but PC couldn't be sure. That, she would believe, though. His long white beard and belly that shook when he laughed like a bowl full of jelly was St. Nick to a tee.

"Alright. Thanks Margret. Got another call. Bye." Tran tapped the screen on his phone. "Hey Doc… you can't tell me over the phone?… okay, we'll be there in a few."

PC squinted. "Dr. Mack?"

"Yeah. He's got the preliminaries on the autopsy. Said I'd need to see it to believe it." He closed his computer and stood.

"I guess it's kind of on the way to my house." Curiosity gnawed at PC, but she didn't want to seem over-eager. She wasn't technically on the case, after all.

"Let's go, then."

Dr. Mack looked up as PC and Tran entered the makeshift morgue. "Couldn't resist the mystery, huh, PC?"

She smiled in answer.

The Medical Examiner led them to a stainless-steel table, where a large, sheet-covered body lay.

Tran's brow furrowed. "Why is it wet around his face?"

"*That* is what I wanted you to see."

Dr. Mack pulled back the sheet to reveal Whit Bulger. White foam oozed from his mouth and nose. There was also some bruising on his face and head that hadn't been visible earlier.

PC moved in for a closer look, then turned back to the ME. "He drowned?"

"Yep. Lungs are full of water."

Tran shook his head and looked from PC to Dr. Mack. "What did I miss? He was found on the floor below the choir loft and the safety rail was broken. But that didn't kill him? He drowned? How does that even work?"

Dr. Mack shrugged. "Your guess is as good as mine. But I don't think this was an accident." He moved to cover the victim's face with the sheet, then stopped. "Oh, there was something else." The ME revealed Bulger's left arm. "I noticed a sticky spot just above his elbow."

Tran peered at the limb. "What is it?"

"Honey."

The officer's brow crinkled. "Where'd that come from?"

Dr. Mack shrugged.

"Jillibella's had a booth at the tree lighting yesterday. I was going to get some sopapillas, but they were sold out. Those are covered in honey," PC said. "I suppose we could go by the restaurant and check credit card receipts. Won't help if he paid in cash, though."

She pulled out her notebook and studied the sketch she'd made yesterday. "Look. There's a huge baptismal pool right up here, at the front of the church. What if Bulger got into a scuffle with our mystery man, fell out of the loft, got the wind knocked out of him, then got dragged over to be drowned? The killer would have moved the body back to make it look like an accident. Or he was drowned first, and the killer broke the railing in the loft afterward. But the drowning explains why his face was clean. His shirt was already wet from firefighting sweat."

Tran cocked his head. "How do you know his face wasn't clean?"

"I saw him at the cottage. He was covered in soot. He had words with someone I didn't see. I didn't actually hear a response, either just Bulger shouting. Said he was going to see Woody. Twenty minutes later, Bulger was dead."

Tran ran his tongue over his front teeth. "I think we should go have another look around Justice Avenue Baptist Church."

"Can you bring me a water sample from the pool while you're there?" Dr. Mack opened a cabinet and retrieved a pint-sized container.

PC took it from him. "See you later, Doc."

As they walked out to Trans's squad, he asked, "What happens if Reverend Costas won't let us look around?"

"It's a death scene in a murder investigation. I don't see he has much choice."

They didn't talk much on the way to the church. Tran rounded the corner onto Justice Avenue and made a left into the parking lot of Justice Avenue Baptist Church. Half of the lot was blocked off with black and white sawhorse type barricades and filled with folding chairs.

Reverend Costas stood on a portable stage at the center front of all the seating. Several people stood at various places in the audience area.

"Testing. Testing. 1-2-3," Costas repeated as he strolled across the stage.

A man in the back row waved his arms. "Too far. You're getting out of range."

Costas took a few steps backward. "Better?"

The man gave a thumbs up.

The reverend turned his attention to PC and Tran as they walked in from the back of the lot. He waited until they were closer than shouting distance before he spoke.

"How can I help Possumwood's finest this morning?"

"Good morning, Reverend." Tran gave him a tight-lipped smile. "We've had some new evidence come to light and we need to take another look at the sanctuary."

"Of course. You can find your own way?"

PC nodded. "Yes, thank you."

Tran marched toward the lobby that fronted the sanctuary. PC paused to examine the outdoor fountain where water poured from the side of a ten-foot bronze Jesus. *If I was going to drown someone in this fountain, no one would ever see me behind this statue. Especially in the dark.*

"Tran. Come over here."

He let go of the door and trotted to the fountain. "Found something?"

"Look at this." PC pointed to a streak of soot on the concrete rim of the pool.

"How about that." He looked toward the door. "Whit Bulger was 250 lbs if he was an ounce. Across the courtyard, through the lobby, then up the aisle to the stage seems like a long way for anybody to move that much dead weight."

"That's true…" PC laid her index finger across her upper lip for a moment. "But military and first responders are trained on the fireman's lift technique. You can carry someone bigger than yourself that way if you do it correctly."

He nodded, chewing the inside of his cheek. "You're right. It's been a while since boot camp. We should still check the baptismal pool."

"Agreed, but someone will have to come back later for a sample. We only have the one container. I don't suppose you have any tape."

"Tape?"

PC dipped her head toward the dark smudge. "To collect some of that soot."

"Bet someone has some on their desk inside."

"Probably. We need a second water sample container, too. I'll grab some water from the fountain." She dipped the pint container into the reservoir.

They stepped inside the church. PC set her water specimen on the closest pulpit. Tran walked up the three steps to the baptismal pool.

"Bet you could get at least ten people in there."

A three-foot wooden gate blocked access to the water from the top step. He tried opening it, but it was locked.

PC looked on. "Somebody might have gotten Bulger over the gate but getting him back out of that water? That pool's what? Three, three and a half feet deep? Not many people are going to be able to deadlift 250 pounds to a height of six feet or more."

"They could have thrown him over the side."

"But the carpet wasn't wet. And if I remember correctly, neither were his pants. Just his shirt. I'm pretty sure he was killed in the fountain."

The church secretary loaned them her tape dispenser so they could collect some soot from the concrete. They dropped off their samples at Dr. Mack's morgue in the back of Clay's Funeral Home, but the Medical Examiner had already left.

Tran started his cruiser. "You ready to go home?"

"Yeah. But could we stop by the cottage? I'd like to see these artifacts."

"Sure thing."

Tran pulled up to the curb in front of the burned-out building. A white car was a dozen yards in front of him. A man and a woman were having such an in-depth discussion that they didn't seem to notice the police car park near them.

PC recognized Dinah Mae Brown's long auburn hair immediately. The tall, trim man leaning against the car took her a minute. Reverend Steve Anders.

The detective leaned forward to get out of the car and stopped. "Hey, Tran? That red and gold sticker on the car—Semper Fi? Isn't that…"

"The Marine Corps."

Chapter 9

Tran tapped his thumb on the steering wheel. "You suppose the Reverend Anders knows how to do a fireman's carry?"

"If he's a marine, probably so." PC reached for the door handle.

Reverend Anders and Dinah Mae noticed them and stopped their intense conversation. PC and Tran exited the cruiser and walked up to the pair.

Dinah Mae smiled and batted her eyelashes. "Afternoon, y'all. Come to see the artifacts?"

"Yes, ma'am," Tran answered.

"Well, come on then. I'll show you." She turned toward her companion. "Steve, you met PC Donovan?"

He tipped his denim cap and extended a meaty paw. "No, I haven't had the pleasure."

PC shook the pastor's hand, and he clapped his other one over her elbow. *Why the power move, Rev?*

Anders let her go and peered at Tran's nametag for a moment. "Officer Tran." The reverend shook his hand vigorously, but without the elbow grab.

Dinah Mae led them to the front door, ducking under the yellow crime scene tape across the porch columns.

"Now y'all be careful, ya hear? Watch your step."

The cottage stank of charred wood and gasoline. A hole had been gouged in a wall across from the fireplace by a firefighter's ax. On the floor lay a tarnished silver brooch set with green stones. PC wasn't sure whether they were rhinestones or peridot. It would be stunning once it was cleaned up. A little further along the wall, the paneling had not only been split, but a section had been removed. A set of silver flatware with gold accents was scattered across the floor in front of the hole.

Dinah Mae gestured to the ruined paneling. "Gotta pull all that wainscottin' down to see if there's anything else in there when they finish their investigatin'. Captain Lopez says he thinks the stonework is stable enough we could just restore the wood, but of course, we'll have to get a structural engineer to confirm that."

PC looked at the silverware. "If your application for declaring this as a historical site is approved, right?"

"Well, of course. Surely it will be. The new State Archaeologist is comin' down to look around tomorrow. Her name's Fairley Cooper."

PC's mind flashed back to the last State Archaeologist who'd come to Possumwood and hoped Dr. Cooper didn't meet Dr. McIlwraith's same grisly fate.

The detective walked over to the area under the window where the arsonist had poured in the gasoline. The closer PC got, the stronger the odor of gas became. Seemed odd that she could smell it—they usually had to bring in sniffer dogs to detect accelerant after a fire. Perhaps there was some on the ground outside the window or on the fieldstone wall.

Did the person who set the fire see the kids sleeping by the hearth before they lit the match?

PC shook her head, staring at the deeply charred floor.

What if Whit Bulger was killed because he saw the arsonist? Did he follow them into the church and try to apprehend them?

If Steve Anders had been in the Marines, he'd have training in hand-to-hand combat. And he's not a small man.

"I think I've seen enough, Dinah Mae. How about you, Tran?"

He nodded, and they all headed to the door.

Steve Anders leaned against one of the posts that held up the roof of the small front porch.

PC glanced at Tran, then turned to Anders. "Reverend, could we speak with you for a few minutes?"

"Of course."

The detective smiled at Dinah Mae. "In private?" PC got out her notebook.

"I'll wait in the car. It's startin' to get chilly out here."

"What can I do you for?" Anders grinned at them.

The detective turned her head toward his car, and his eyes followed. "That *Semper Fi* sticker on your car. Were you—"

"Six years. Field medic."

"Thank you for your service." She gave a little nod. "Did you have much interaction with Whit Bulger during the run-up to the cantata?"

Anders pursed his lips and shook his head slightly. "Not really. I wasn't singing, so I didn't go to cantata practice. Unfortunately, I did see him occasionally at organizational meetings. Only had a need for a bail bond that one time."

"Sorry about your brother. That must have been hard," Tran remarked.

"Still is. But thanks for your concern."

"When did you arrive at the tree lighting yesterday?" PC's pen hovered over the page.

"Around 11:00. It started at noon, but I helped Dinah Mae set up the Historical Society booth. We sold raffle tickets to raise money to stabilize the tunnels downtown so we can give tours."

"How long were you there?"

"I took a dinner break around six, then went over to the gazebo for the cantata preview."

"And that started at seven." PC said, primarily for her own benefit.

Plenty of time to eat, set the fire, and return. "Did you eat with anyone, Reverend?"

Anders shook his head. "No. Just wandered around looking at the vendors."

Flimsy alibi. "What did you do when the fire started?"

"I'm one of the volunteer firefighters, so I ran over there to help put it out."

Most people don't suspect the firemen, but a surprising number are arsonists.

"And once the flames were quenched, what did you do?"

"As I told you earlier, I waited with Chief Lopez until the DPS investigators arrived."

"So you did. Refresh my memory. What time was that again?"

"Late. I think around 10:00."

PC closed her notebook. "Thank you for your time, Reverend."

PC walked with the pastor to his car and Tran followed. She smiled at Dinah Mae. "Talk to you later." She turned and headed toward the cruiser.

As soon as they were inside, Tran frowned. "Shouldn't we talk with her now?"

"No. If she's covering something up, I want to give her the opportunity to sweat."

"Dinah Mae? Surely you mean perspire." Tran reached for his seatbelt. "What do you think about Steve Anders?"

"He blames Whit for his brother's death, but if there was a trigger for him to act, it hasn't come to light. He has military training and he's a big ole boy. He doesn't have a solid alibi for the time the fire was set. Looks like a good suspect, but there's no hard evidence. We should talk to the fire chief to confirm his story about being there until DPS arrived. If he really was at the cottage until ten, that removes his opportunity to kill Whit. Still could have set the fire, though. The murderer and the arsonist might be two different people who may or may not be working together."

"If we're interviewing witnesses, then Paula Stein is an

obvious candidate. We took her statement yesterday at the hospital, but she wasn't in much condition to talk. Supposed to have been released this morning."

"Good idea."

"Still want me to drop you at the house, or do you wanna come?"

PC glanced at her FlitBit. It was hours before the critters would be expecting dinner. "I guess I could go along."

Tran shifted into drive. "Let me fill you in on what she told us. The cottage is three rooms, right? The living room where the fire started, a bedroom that was parallel to it and shared a wall with the fireplace, and a narrow room that isn't much more than a hallway that ran along the end of the house and joined the other two rooms together. Mrs. Stein and her oldest child, Sarina, were in the bedroom. There was no window, so they could have lights on in there without being seen from the outside. Sarina was doing homework and Paula was reading."

"Did they hear or see anyone?"

"No. Adam, the youngest, came running in, apparently had a bad dream. Next thing they knew, there was smoke everywhere. They were able to get the middle daughter into the bedroom with them, but they couldn't get out because the only door was blocked by flames. They all got on the floor, trying to avoid the smoke."

"That must have been terrifying."

Tran nodded, and they drove on.

PC stared out the window. Whit Bulger drowned. That explains why there was no scream. No one would seriously try to commit suicide from a ten-foot height. If he had actually fallen, he would have made some kind of noise. A curse at the person who pushed him. A shout of surprise when he crashed through the railing. A thud when he hit the floor below. That was one mystery explained.

Perhaps Paula Stein would have some answers.

If it wasn't her abusive husband who tried to kill her and her children, who was it?

Chapter 10

Tran knocked on the front door of Paula Stein's house, the fresh evergreen Christmas wreath vibrating with each blow and giving off its resinous perfume.

"Who is it?" asked a female voice from inside.

"Possumwood PD," Tran answered. "We'd like to talk to Paula Stein."

The door opened, revealing a forty-ish woman with haunted eyes and wispy blonde hair. "Come in."

She closed the door. "Have you caught him?"

"Him?" PC asked.

Paula raised an eyebrow. "My ex-husband? The one who tried to kill us?"

"I'm sorry, but Mr. Stein was in the drunk tank in the Tulsa City Jail at the time of the fire." Tran answered. "We were hoping you could provide us with a little more information."

"But Darcy said…" The homeowner frowned.

"Who's Darcy?" PC asked.

"Would you like some iced tea or anything?"

"No, thanks." Tran shook his head.

"A bottle of water would be nice, if you have any." PC replied.

Paula gestured to the sofa as she disappeared into the kitchen. She returned with two water bottles and handed one to PC before she sat down in the loveseat. Tran and PC sat on the couch.

"Darcy is Jeff's sister. She and I always got along. She knows exactly what her brother is capable of, even if his mama won't see it. Jeff moved back home after he got outta jail the last time. Darcy gives me a heads up if he's headed back this way. She called and said he was comin'.'"

"How long had you been staying at the cottage?" Tran asked.

"We only hid there when Jeff was around." She gave a bitter laugh. "It's not like I was gonna pull the kids outta school to hole up in some abandoned shack full time. And Darcy said Jeff had a girlfriend, so even when he came lookin' for us, he didn't try too hard or stay too long."

PC pulled out her notebook and wrote a few things down. "Mrs. Stein, would you tell us about last night?"

Paula opened her water and took a long drink. "Darcy called me Thursday afternoon to say he was plannin' on leavin' Friday to come wish us happy late Thanksgiving. Guess he made a pit stop at Angel's Bar."

She snorted. "It's an all-day drive from Tulsa to here, and I was pretty sure he wasn't gettin' up at the crack of dawn. We ate an early supper at Zeno's Pizza Friday night and headed to the cottage afterward, when it was good and dark. Probably 6:30 or 7."

The detective nodded. "And how long were you planning to stay?"

"Figgered he'd be gone by Sunday. But I'd give Thea—she lives next door—a call first to make sure he wasn't hangin' around. We'd come back early enough to get cleaned up and get to church, if the coast was clear. But nothing happened Saturday, until the fire. And you know about that."

PC turned a page in her notebook. "I'd like to hear what you saw that evening."

"That's just it. I didn't see anything. Sarina and I were in the bedroom, because it doesn't have windows and we could have a light. I did smell smoke, but it's chilly, and people have their fireplaces goin'. I didn't realize what was happenin', not until Adam came runnin' in."

"I see." PC clicked her pen closed and open again. "Do you mind if we speak with the children? They might have noticed something you didn't."

Paula shrugged. "I guess."

The detective uncrossed her ankles. "If we could see them one at a time, that would be perfect. And of course, you need to be here."

"Belle! Honey, can you come in the livin' room for a minute?"

A moment later, a preteen girl with a blonde bob trotted in. She stopped short when she saw the policeman.

"Baby, come sit with me. Detective Donovan and Officer Tran here want to talk to you about last night."

The girl shook her head. "I was asleep. Don't remember

anything. Not 'til you dragged me into the bedroom. Then Makayla's dad came and got us. Can I go? Sarah and I are makin' a video."

PC nodded.

"Alright, baby. Send your brother in."

He must have been lurking in the hallway, listening, because Belle said, "Don't just stand there. Go see Mama."

He crept into the room, holding a plastic dinosaur between himself and the visitors.

PC gave him her warmest smile. She remembered when her nephew, Tyson, had gone through his dinosaur phase. "Hi. I'm Detective Donovan. My friend here is Officer Tran. What's your name?"

His shoulders hunched, and he looked at the floor. "Adam."

"It's good to meet you, Adam. What kind of dino you got there? Is that a T-Rex?"

He shook his head and looked up at her as if she'd asked if it was a Barbie doll. "No! It's a Saurophaganax. It's bigger than a T-Rex."

"Really? They hadn't found any of those when I was your age."

"You must be really old."

"Adam!" Paula gave her son a sharp glare.

"Sorry."

PC chuckled. "Speaking of really old things, would you tell me about being in the cabin last night?"

"I hate it there."

PC nodded sympathetically. "It's hard sleeping away from home sometimes. Even for grownups."

Adam leaned toward PC. "There was a young corythosaurus there. Mama didn't believe me, but I saw it!"

Paula sighed. "Adam. The dinosaurs have all been dead for a long, long time."

"This one wasn't! It might have crawled out from under the house. It was very noisy. That's what woke me up. Then I saw it looking in the window at me."

"I see." PC tapped the page with her pen. *Did he see the arsonist, or just have a bad dream?* "Would you describe what you saw?"

"It was dark. I didn't get a super good look at it. It wasn't tall enough to be a full-grown corythosaur, so it must have been a kid."

"And what did it look like?" Tran asked.

"Well… the outline was kinda like a giant duck—that's why they call them duck-billed dinosaurs. But it wasn't a duck. It didn't have wings. Arms." He nodded for emphasis and raised his hands. "Definitely arms—it opened the window. I shouldn't have been scared. They're herbivores." He cast his eyes miserably to the floor.

"If I saw a dinosaur coming in my window, I'd have been scared, too. No matter what it eats," PC reassured him.

Adam perked up a little.

Paula stroked her son's hair. "I'm sure whatever you heard under the house was just an armadillo, or a raccoon.

Nothing scarier than that. You were half asleep and imagined seein' a dinosaur."

"But mom…"

PC's eyes fell on the plastic toy he held. "Adam? Do you have a model of this cory—what was it again?"

"Corythosaurus. I have a book about hadrosaurs. I'll go get it."

He returned moments later with a hardcover illustrated book and sat on the couch between PC and Tran. Adam flipped through the pages until he got to an entry for corythosaurus.

"There. See?" His finger tapped a drawing.

The creature stood upright on its hind limbs. Its arms, although longer and more developed than a T-Rex's, were still small. A bony crest topped its head, and it had a flattish, narrow snout. *It did look a great deal like a duck… or a man in a cap, seen in silhouette.*

"Thank you, Adam. That's very helpful." PC snapped a picture with her phone. "I'll never be able to make that good of a drawing, and I need it for my records."

The boy's face lit up.

"Thank you for talking to us. You've been a big help."

"Alright, honey. You run along, now. Tell Sarina to come in here, please."

The cowed boy who'd crept into the living room a few minutes ago walked out, book under his arm and head held high.

It took some time for a petite teenager to wander in.

Dark circles underscored her large brown eyes, and her cheeks were blotchy. She was the girl with the hot pink hair that Whit Bulger's daughter helped out of the cottage.

PC smiled. "You must be Sarina."

"Yes."

"I'm Detective Donovan and this is Officer Tran. We're trying to catch the person who hurt Makayla's dad."

"You mean murdered him?"

"Yes." PC bit her lip. She hadn't switched gears quickly enough between young child and teen, and she hoped Sarina didn't hold it against her. "We don't know if there's a connection to the fire, but there might be. Is there anything you remember from last night that might help? Did you see or hear anything unusual?"

"No. I was doing my homework. Had my earbuds in, listening to music."

PC turned the page in her notebook. "What about Makayla? Had she been at the cottage?"

Sarina's eyes darted toward the back door. "No. She was going to come by after the singing. She was at the Episcopal Church that afternoon."

Tran's brow wrinkled. "What was she doing there? I thought the Bulgers were Catholic."

Sarina contemplated the area rug, as if she were tracing the concentric ovals in her mind.

Paula's eyes locked with her daughter's. "You should tell 'em. It may help."

The teenager sighed. "Reverend Wholt is a graphic

designer. Makala wanted to learn about graphic designing to make her socials better and get more followers."

"Her socials?" Tran asked.

"Social media. Keep up, Zoomer. You're supposed to speak the lingo." PC answered, so Sarina didn't have to.

"Millennial," Tran muttered *almost* under his breath.

Sarina crossed her arms. "Yeah. She went to the church after school on Tuesdays and Thursdays. Last week was Thanksgiving, so they had the thing on Saturday. It was legit. He wasn't creepin' on her or anything. There were always people around—she wasn't the only one he was teaching. Sometimes, I took the class with her."

Sarina closed her eyes and swallowed hard. "Her dad found out." Her lips tightened. "Instead of giving her credit for taking initiative—and he's always goin' on and on about that—he grounded her."

Tran cocked his head. "Why do you think that was?"

"He didn't trust her to run her own life. He had to control everything she did." Sarina scowled.

PC shifted her weight. "Was it her he didn't trust, or the pastor?"

Sarina's eyebrow shot up. "She was the one who got punished."

I wonder.

"Is that all?"

"Unless you can think of anything else." PC clicked her pen closed.

Sarina drifted into the kitchen, and Paula sighed.

PC stood up. "She's been through a lot since yesterday. You all have. Don't be too hard on them. Or yourself."

Tran followed her example. "Thanks for your time, Mrs. Stein. You don't have to worry about your ex for quite a while. I don't see him getting out of jail any time soon."

"Thank goodness for that."

She showed them to the door and waved goodbye. PC and Tran got into his cruiser.

He started the car. "You wanna grab some lunch?"

She checked her FlitBit. It was after 1:00. "Sure. Didn't realize it was so late."

"Lucky Wok?"

"You get a family discount?" PC grinned.

"Nope. But we both get a law enforcement discount."

She chuckled. He drove to his in-laws' restaurant.

Tran pulled the door of his cruiser shut and rubbed his belly. "I always eat way too much there." He buckled his seatbelt. "Do you suppose Reverend Wholt is still at the church? It's almost 2:00."

"One way to find out."

St. Mark's Episcopal Church wasn't far. Two cars sat in the parking lot.

"Looks like somebody's here," PC said.

They got out and went in search of an open door. One next to the sanctuary was unlocked, and they walked inside.

"Hello?" PC called. "Reverend Wholt?"

A woman PC guessed to be in her mid-60s stepped into the corridor. "Is there something I can do for you?"

"Yes, ma'am," Tran purred. "We'd like to see Reverend Wholt, if he's available."

She gestured to the doorway. "Yes. He's in here."

The woman returned to the room. PC and Tran followed.

The man sitting behind a large wooden desk looked up and got to his feet when they entered the office. He was under six feet tall and fine-boned. Probably didn't weigh 150 lbs soaking wet. He'd need a winch and a wheelbarrow to move Whit Bulger's body.

"I'm Thomas Wholt. How can I help you?"

"We'd like to speak with you about Whit Bulger," Tran said.

"Terrible tragedy, even if he did threaten to kill me."

Chapter 11

"Oh?" Tran tilted his head. "Why did Whit Bulger threaten to kill you?"

The minister sat back down. "I don't wish to speak ill of the dead."

"Not even if it could help catch his killer?" PC asked.

Thomas Wholt gestured to some chairs in front of his desk. "I had heard it was an accident."

Tran chose the seat farthest from the door. PC sat and pulled her chair as close to the desk as possible. "Someone went to a lot of trouble to make it look that way."

"Oh, dear. My heart goes out to his family."

PC nodded. "You knew Makayla, right?"

The minister hesitated. "Yes."

Tran leaned forward. "How did you know her?"

Wholt rearranged some papers on his desk. "What Mr. Bulger did was uncalled for. But I can understand. Some members of the clergy have been… inappropriate with children. Not most of us. But, as they say, a few rotten apples spoil the whole barrel. He thought he was protecting his daughter."

PC gave him an encouraging nod.

The pastor pursed his lips. "Makayla had come to me to ask some questions about graphic design. She and Sarina Stein are best friends, so Sarina came along more often than not, although she didn't come with Makayla yesterday. It wasn't just the girls. Several business owners were interested in improving their branding on a shoestring budget, so I started having informal classes on Tuesday and Thursday afternoons. Karla Fitzroy, from Karla's Kurls, was one of them."

"That's very civic-minded of you." Tran tucked his thumbs into his belt.

"What doth it profit, my brethren, though a man say he hath faith, and have not works? Can faith save him? Faith, if it hath not works, is dead."

PC clenched her jaw and let it go. Putting the preacher on the defensive was not going to get him to open up. "So, Reverend Wholt? What happened between you and Whit Bulger?"

Wholt picked up his pen. "We were just finishing up the class. The Christmas tree lighting festival would be starting soon. Whit came barging in, looking for Makayla."

The pastor set his pen down, then moved it to another spot on his desk.

Tran started to say something, but PC kicked him in the ankle. Not hard enough to hurt. Much.

"It turned out," Wholt said, "that she hadn't been entirely truthful about where she was spending the morning. Whit had told her to go to the office and help her mother."

PC pulled out her notebook. "I can see why he'd be upset if he didn't know where she was."

"Nancy—that's Makayla's mother—was aware of the classes. I'm not sure Whit was. They weren't very busy at City Bail Bonds that day, so Nancy told her to go home. Mom thought she was home, Dad thought she was at work. She failed to mention she was coming here. Not sure if it was intentional, or just an oversight."

The detective shifted in her chair. "Did Whit threaten you?"

"Yes. But I don't think he meant it." Wholt moved his pen again. "Something you have to understand about Whit. He was a control freak. Which made him the perfect guy to wrangle singers from five different churches into one cohesive choir. So, you see, I'm not criticizing. Not at all. And it did save his life."

Tran's brow crinkled. "How so?"

The minister leaned back in his chair and scrutinized Tran, then PC. "You don't know much about Whit, do you?"

PC smiled. "That's why we're talking to people who knew him."

Wholt picked up his pen, then tapped it on the desk. "You are aware he served time for second degree murder, right?"

What? PC nodded and mumbled noncommittally.

The pastor continued. "He was twenty-one. He'd fallen in with a rough crowd. There was a house party. Lots of alcohol involved. Whit thought a young man was trying to steal his wallet. No telling if that's what really happened—by all accounts, everyone was highly inebriated. This young man ended up being shot dead. Nobody admitted anything about where the gun came from, but it was never found. The kicker is, Whit may or may not have been the killer. He might have taken the fall for someone else. He never said that himself, but Nancy implied it once."

Tran leaned forward. "Any idea who he was protecting?"

Wholt shook his head. "Happened long before I arrived in Possumwood. And as harsh as it may sound, being sent to prison was probably the best thing to happen to Whit. It led him to God. The man who walked out of prison was very different from the boy who entered. It was his iron-fisted control that kept him on the straight and narrow while he was paying his debt to society."

PC scrubbed a hand down her face, then rested her jaw on her palm for a moment. "How do you know all of this stuff about Whit?"

"He came to our church and told us. He has given many motivational speeches throughout the area. There's a speaker page on his website. I'm sure he'd have been happy to do a presentation for the police."

Tran's eyes slid to PC and back to Wholt. "Then I guess the system works."

"Sometimes. Sometimes it does."

PC studied the bruise underneath the pastor's eye, then rubbed her cheekbone. "What happened to you?"

Wholt looked at the desk and covered his eyes for a moment. "Of course you were going to ask me that. I was chaperoning the youth fellowship trip to the roller rink in Horice on Friday. Something to keep the kids occupied while their parents hit the sales. They wanted me to skate with them." He shook his head. "I haven't skated since I was in elementary school. The floor and I got to be good friends. Not my finest hour."

The detective put away her notebook. "Reverend, do you know of anyone who might have been angry with Whit?"

"Angry enough to kill him?"

Tran eyed the preacher. "Someone did."

The pastor rubbed his chin absently. "No one specific, but of course, his job brought him into daily contact with people on the wrong side of the law."

"Thank you for your time, Reverend Wholt." PC tucked her notebook into her bag and rose.

Tran also stood, and the two of them walked out to his squad. Once they were in the car, PC turned to Tran.

"Did you have any idea Bulger had done time?"

"No. Never had any reason to look into his background, before now. And I didn't even know he gave motivational speeches."

"Me, either. It might be helpful to check into his past a bit before talking to his family. We're way behind on the victimology. What do you think about Wholt as a suspect?"

The officer shook his head. "He may have had opportunity, but not motive, and definitely not means."

"I agree. Maybe—"

Tran's text chime sounded, and he looked at his phone. He typed in a response and slipped the device back into his pocket before shifting the car into reverse.

"That's the Chief. He's about to go home and wants an update."

"Let's give it to him."

Woody leaned back in his battered leather executive chair. Officer Charles Bourgeois sat in one of the two Naugahyde and steel chairs in front of the Chief's desk. When Tran and PC entered the office, he got to his feet. In his haste, he knocked over a framed photo on Woody's desk.

"See y'all later." Bourgeois hustled out the door.

PC's eyes fell on the picture. It was a fading 5 x 7 of a teenage Woody and his cousin, Clem Wilson, standing next to the sign for the Mirabella County Fair and Rodeo. She had known Clem in passing, but they weren't close by any stretch of the imagination. He was a couple of years older and had dropped out of school.

Each boy grinned as he held the lead of a fluffy white Charolais steer. A third boy stood between them, holding a calf roping lariat. He smiled underneath a shock of curly blond hair.

His face… could that be Whit Bulger? Knew he and Woody were friends but didn't realize they went that far back.

The Chief stood the photo back up, facing it away from the visitors' chairs.

"How're you feeling, Woody?" PC sat in the chair recently vacated by Bourgeois.

Tran took the other. Chief Wilson rubbed his temple.

"Like something the cat dragged in. Donovan, you interested in coming out of retirement?"

"Not really. Why?"

"Gorman's on indefinite leave. Now Bourgeois is planning to retire in March. They're my most senior officers. Bourgeois was here when I started. Anyway. Consider yourself on the payroll for this one. What's the update?"

Tran cleared his throat. "Seems like Bulger rubbed a lot of people the wrong way. But so far, the only person who might have been able to drown him in the fountain—"

"I'm sorry. Did you say, 'drown him?' I must have misheard."

PC shook her head. "No. You heard correctly. Dr. Mack said he drowned. We looked in the fountain reservoir and the baptismal pool. There was soot on the edge of the fountain and the baptismal was locked. I think whoever killed Bulger tried to stage it to look like an accident by putting the body under the choir loft and breaking the railing."

Tran continued. "Reverend Steve Anders has the most reason to kill Bulger—he wouldn't give a bail bond to Anders' brother, and he got killed in jail waiting on his trial. He's also big enough to possibly overpower Bulger and move the body. And he *is* former military."

"There is… something else." PC leaned forward. "After the fire was put out, Whit yelled at someone—they were on the other side of the house, and I couldn't see who it was. Then he told me he was on his way to see you. Seems weird he ended up dead twenty minutes later at the Justice Avenue Baptist Church on the opposite side of town."

Woody shook his head. "He never made it here."

"I didn't think so."

The Chief closed his eyes and leaned his head on his hand. "I'm done for the day."

PC bit her lip. "You don't look so good. We're gonna take you to Hilda's house."

"Then I wouldn't have a vehicle."

"I can drive you there in your Tahoe, Tran can follow and pick me up. You look like you're about to pass out at any second, and I don't think you should be behind the wheel."

"She's right," Tran added.

Woody opened his mouth and closed it several times. Then he exhaled loudly. "Fine."

He rose and tossed PC his keys.

The conference room chair squeaked as PC sat down, setting her cup on the table. Woody had been dropped off at his mother's house and PC's stale-when-she-got-it coffee was cooling while she waited for the creaky Possumwood PD laptop to boot up. Finally, it kicked in and she was able to access the internet.

She scoured the City Bail Bonds' website. There was, indeed, a speaker's page. She read through his bio and the testimonials. Unsurprisingly, everyone gushed about Bulger's amazing Cinderella story. PC chided herself for being too jaded. He deserved credit for getting his life together.

Next, she researched his criminal history. The incident at the house party happened two years after she'd graduated from Possumwood High School and left for college. Not surprising that she hadn't heard about it.

The address of the murder was 934 Whispering Oaks Lane.

Why does that address seem familiar?

She took a long swig of lukewarm coffee.

Wait. Isn't Whispering Oaks the subdivision where the gun was found buried under the driveway back in June?

She got to her feet and searched for the file. The address where the water main had ruptured and blown out the driveway was 2007 Willow Bend Drive. She opened a mapping application in her browser.

PC located 934 Whispering Oaks. It was four blocks from 2007 Willow Bend Drive. She swallowed hard, then returned to the incident report.

The result made her queasy.

The person who had been murdered at the house party all those years ago was Clem Wilson.

Chapter 12

Stunned, PC leaned back in her squeaky chair. *I had no idea Clem was gone. Poor Woody. He must have been devastated. Guess there's not a reason anyone would have notified me. But still…*

She checked the Mirabella County Appraisal District website. The Willow Bend house was built the same year as Clem's murder. The Whispering Oaks one four before that. Clem had been shot with a .357, the same caliber as the driveway gun. Coincidence is not causation, but in her experience, coincidences were few and far between.

It was also true that what she knew and what she could prove were sometimes two different things.

The detective shook her head and sighed. "I guess that means that gun probably had nothing to do with Daddy's murder," she remarked to the screen.

A lump rose in her throat. Wonder if Woody was at that party?

She reached for her phone to text him but reconsidered. He needed to rest right now and asking about Clem's death would only upset him. But the idea that Whit Bulger might have been protecting someone gnawed at her. Worst-case scenarios popped up in her mind like mushrooms. What she needed was facts. And she had no access to anything that even resembled evidence right now.

Wholt had said that Nancy once implied that Whit took the fall, willingly or not, for the real killer. Who had been at the party? The only two people she was certain had been there were both dead. While she was wracking her brain to come up with anyone who a) ran in that circle, b) might have been in Possumwood at that time, and c) was in Possumwood now, Tran knocked on the doorframe.

"You wanna go talk to the Bulgers?"

PC blinked a few times while she mentally shifted gears. "Nancy and Makayla? Sure."

She stared out the window as Tran drove down Justice Avenue. Crews had been busy adding wreaths with red bows to the streetlights. Gold tinsel garland shimmered in the light breeze where it spanned the street above stop lights. Poinsettias bloomed from drifts of fiber fill snow in shop windows.

Perhaps it was beginning to look a lot like Christmas, but she wasn't much feeling it. Perhaps once Whit Bulger's murder was solved…

Tran hung a left at Justice Lutheran Church and headed toward Independence Road, where he turned right. The decorations stopped abruptly north of Justice Avenue. Independence Road was the northern border of Possumwood, a twenty-four-foot strip of asphalt that separated farmland from the town. A few blocks later, he turned left again.

On the right side of the gravel road stood a classic white farmhouse with a wide front porch. A thick line of evergreens formed a windbreak on the north side. A handful of chickens, feathers puffed out for warmth, meandered through the yard. A large, very hairy, yellow dog lifted his grizzled muzzle from his fluffy bed near the door and barked when they pulled into the driveway.

The storm door opened, and a woman stood on the front porch. PC guessed it was Nancy Bulger. The detective hesitated to get out of the car, but the dog didn't get up.

The woman craned her neck, trying to get a good view of both of them. "Do you have any news?"

"I'm sorry, Mrs. Bulger. Not yet. But we wanted to clarify some things. This is Detective Donovan."

Nancy nodded and held the door open as they came up the walk. She looked at the dog. "It's okay, Taffy. They're friends."

PC eyed the curled-up canine as she stepped onto the porch.

"Don't worry about him, Detective. He's half blind and barely has any teeth. He's old, but he's still a good boy. Aren't you, Taffy?"

His tail thumped on the dog bed.

The three stepped inside, the door banging behind them.

Nancy sighed, her eyes puffy and ringed with dark circles. "How can I help you?"

"We'd like to speak with Makayla, if possible." Tran looked around the room.

"I'm not sure that's a good idea. She's really struggling with her father's death."

PC shifted her weight. "I understand how difficult this is. We're doing everything we can to catch the person who did this. But we need to ask your daughter a couple of questions. It won't take long."

"Okay. Have a seat." Nancy gestured to a blue sectional. "I'll get her."

They each claimed a big, square cushion. While they were waiting, PC got out her notebook and looked around the room. The house was open plan, and she could see into the kitchen. A red enamel kettle sat on the cooktop. On the counter nearby was a mug with a tea bag tab hanging out of it. Next to that was a jar of a dark golden-brown liquid. She remembered the distinctive label from the tea booth yesterday.

"Makayla'll be out in a minute."

PC hadn't even heard Nancy come back in. "I see you have some *Heidi's Honey*. I bought some yesterday at the tree lighting. Is she from around here?"

"Yeah. She lives about a mile up the road, actually. She and her husband, Ned. Heidi's a bee charmer. And I mean that. Her bees are so happy they make almost twice as much honey as you'd expect. She says it's the buckwheat they grow for the bees." Nancy looked at the side of the sectional for a moment. "Wasn't the best singer, but she'd been coming over once a week to get lessons from Whit so she could be in the Christmas cantata."

"That was very kind of him," Tran said.

"Yes, I think so. She's kind of mousy, and Ned is, well, domineering. She's spent the night here a few times, when she couldn't deal with his demands."

"Oh?" PC unzipped her bag. *Do we have a jealous husband in the mix now?*

"She's a sweet kid. I've suggested she might be better off somewhere else. Somewhere away from Ned."

Looks like we need to go see Ned, then.

Makayla moped into the room and slumped into the recliner. She looked so fragile that PC just wanted to hug her and tell her everything would be okay. Instead, she said, "Makayla? This is Officer Tran, and I'm Detective Donovan." She gave the teen a little kind smile. "We'd like to ask you a few questions."

"Sure." Makayla looked anything but sure.

PC folded her hands in her lap. "We're so sorry for your loss. But we'd really appreciate it if you can help us out with a little information."

Makayla raised a skeptical eyebrow. "What about?"

"Can we clear something up?" Tran jumped in.

"What's that?"

"Did you take the quilts off the clothesline at the Afters? And raid their veggie patch to feed the Steins?" Tran's eyebrows raised.

PC cleared her throat. She wasn't close enough to Tran to nudge him. Or kick him.

The girl crossed her arms. "And I took some socks, too. The little kids needed them. What of it?"

He leaned back against the chair. "Just for future reference, ask first. Most people will be glad to help you."

"I had to keep it secret. No one could know where they were. Sarina's dad… he can seem incredibly nice, then turn right around and punch you in the face. I didn't want to take the chance that he'd find out their location from someone who thought they were helping."

"I think you made a good choice," PC said. "We'll worry about the quilts later. I'd like to hear everything you did on Saturday."

"Why?"

"Because you might have seen something, or heard something, and not realized that it was important."

Makayla's lips pursed. "And how do you know what's important?"

"That's the thing. Sometimes you just can't tell if something's important until it is."

The girl shrugged. "Whatever. I was grounded because my dad had a fit that I was taking graphic design lessons with Reverend Wholt and some other people and didn't report my exact location at every hour of the day."

A tear welled in her eye and trickled down her cheek.

"After my parents finally left to go to the tree lighting, I got some food together for Sarina and them's dinner. I rode my bike over and saw fire coming out of one window. Called 9-1-1 and reported it. The front door handle was hot, so I was afraid to open it. A backdraft would be worse than leaving it alone."

Tran cocked his head. "How do you know about backdrafts?"

"My dad was a firefighter. Remember?"

Tran's shoulders dropped.

"Anyway, I was banging on the wall where the bedroom was, trying to wake them up, but I couldn't tell if they heard me. Our neighbor, Ned Koehler, was one of the first to get there. I told him about Sarina's family being in the house. I didn't think he knew them, but he looked really upset. As soon as the fire was out enough, I ran inside to get them."

Tran picked at his thumbnail. "You didn't tell your dad?"

Makayla shook her head and sniffled. "He was already on the line. I couldn't tell which one he was. When their equipment's on, they all look alike."

PC leaned forward. "Makayla, think back very carefully. When you were at the house waiting for the fire to be put out, did you see anything unusual? Anyone who seemed out of place?"

"No." She sniffled again.

PC clicked her pen. "I think that's enough. Thank you so much for talking to us, Makayla."

She nodded.

Nancy opened the door for them.

Once they were in the cruiser, Tran put his hands on the wheel. "Now what?"

"Where did you learn your interrogation techniques?"

"What do you mean?"

PC rubbed her eyes. "First of all, it's not your job to try to parent the witness. Patrol policing is different from detective work, and if you're going to wear both hats, you need to be clear on the difference."

"I was just trying to—"

"I'm aware of what you were trying to do. When you

want someone to give you information, make it easy for them. I don't care if you're sitting next to Ted Bundy or Charles Manson, you have to be their non-judgmental best friend, then get out of the way and let them talk. What they tell you may make you sick to your stomach, but you just smile and nod, then throw up later, *after* you've gotten the confession."

"Until this year, there were years between murders here in Possumwood."

"Are you going to blame this crime wave on me, too?"

Tran sucked in a deep breath, then let it out slowly. "Of course not."

The detective stared out the window for a moment, corralling her thoughts. "Do you suppose Dinah Mae is still guarding those artifacts in the cottage?"

"Does a dragon guard a hoard?"

PC clicked her seatbelt. "We should drop by and see if she needs some lunch."

"Closer to dinner."

The detective checked her FlitBit. He was right. "I need to see if my brother can feed Mama's animals." She dialed his number.

"What's up, sis?"

"Rocky, you at home?"

"Yeah...?"

"Look, I'm working on the Bulger case, and I may be home a little late. Can you feed the critters? Instructions are taped to the wall in the feed room."

"I guess."

"And take Cordie out to pee."

"Anything else?"

"Make sure to stay on Arthur's right side. He's blind on the left."

"That it?"

"Yes. Thanks, I owe you."

"You bet."

PC hung up.

Tran pulled up to the curb and parked. There were no cars at the burned-out cottage.

He tapped the steering wheel with his thumbs. "Now what?"

"Let's have a look around."

PC got out of the car and walked up the flagstone path. Yellow tape wrapped the columns that held up the porch roof and sealed the front door. Or what was left of it anyway. It hung by one hinge. Tran followed as she turned and walked around to the bedroom side of the house. In the center of the fieldstone wall, and at ground level, was an ornate wrought iron filigree grating. It was about two feet wide and one tall. It had been painted white at one time, but rust had bled through the paint, staining it brownish orange.

"Whatcha lookin' at?"

She bent and tugged on it. The metal was firmly fixed in place. "You remember Adam Stein said a monster came out from under the house and looked in the window?"

Tran nodded.

PC wiped her hands on her pants. "These grates allow airflow under the building, and they're supposed to keep varmints out. There should be at least two more."

They made their way around to the back and PC tried the grate there. No movement.

"Third time's a charm?" she muttered as they walked around to the living room side.

Light splashed over Tran's squad as a car pulled up behind it.

"Well, speak of the Devil." PC started toward the new arrivals.

Steve Anders got out from behind the wheel and Dinah Mae climbed out of the passenger side.

She batted her eyelashes. "Hey, y'all! Any developments?"

Tran shook his head. "Nothing we can talk about."

Anders grinned. "That's good, right? It means you have something."

Dinah Mae leaned against the car. "What brings y'all back out here?"

"Just chasing down a few leads." PC stepped closer, encroaching on Dinah Mae's personal space. "Since you're here, we may as well talk, right?"

Dinah Mae's eyes were suddenly guarded. "I suppose so." She moved back a step.

PC didn't follow her. "What time did you say you got

here last night?"

Anders crossed his arms. "Is this really necessary? Do you think Dinah Mae had something to do with the murder?"

"Of course not!" PC smiled. "I'm just trying to find out if anybody saw or heard anything unusual."

Dinah Mae shared a look with her companion before she continued. "I was not at the tree lightin'. Steve called me... I think it was 8:30. By the time I got ready and made it here, it was probably 9:00, maybe a little later."

PC pulled out her notebook and paged through it. "That's interesting, because Reverend Anders said that he called you after the DPS team arrived at ten."

The pastor's arms dropped to his sides. "Well, uh. I must have just gotten the time wrong."

Tran tapped the back window of Anders' car with his flashlight. "What's in the back seat, there?"

Dinah Mae took in a long breath of air, her mouth forming a little 'o.'

Anders shrugged. "It's nothing. Just some stuff from the rummage sale yesterday."

PC brightened. "Did you get some good bargains? Let's have a look. I never made it over there."

"Well... um... there's some very personal items in there."

Dinah Mae let out an exasperated sigh and cut her eyes up to the heavens. "Oh, can it, Steve. We're caught."

Reluctantly, he moved out of the way. Tran opened the

door and pulled out a large cardboard box, setting it on the trunk. He held the flashlight while PC opened it.

It was loaded with artifacts, each tagged with a coded adhesive sticker. *From the museum? This where her 'new finds' came from?*

But one item stopped her breath. It wasn't large, but it weighed an emotional ton.

At the bottom of the pile lay the black and white mosaic box that had been stolen the night of Trey Donovan's murder.

Chapter 13

"Where did you get this?" PC struggled to keep her voice calm.

"Get what, sugar?" Dinah Mae peered into the cardboard container.

"This." PC touched the black and white box. A chill ran up her arm and down her spine.

"I found it at a rummage sale. Few years ago. Could tell it was real old, but I couldn't connect it to a particular household here in Possumwood. That's why I never put it out on display."

"I don't suppose there's any way to tell who brought it to the sale?" PC was grasping at straws.

"No." A lock of chestnut hair fell over Dinah Mae's shoulder as she tilted her head. "Does it mean anything to you?"

PC swallowed and took a deep breath. "My father bought that box when he went to the Middle East on business. He had it at the store. Used it to collect donations for the children's hospital. Whoever killed him took it."

"Oh, sugar. I'm so sorry." Dinah Mae picked it up and held it out to PC. "Here. You take it."

The detective stretched her fingers, hoping to stop her hands from shaking as she reached for the mosaic box. She wanted to laugh. To scream. To cry. But she did none of those things. She rolled her emotions into a tight little ball and stuffed them into the same compartment she shoved her feelings when she investigated any horrific crime. Or had to give a death notification to a terrified parent.

"Thank you." PC took the box in both hands, hoping no one noticed the tremor in her fingers.

Tran tapped the cardboard. "Dinah Mae? Care to explain?"

The redhead rubbed PC's arm before she turned to the officer. "We were just givin' the application for our historical site a little boost, that's all. Maybe these artifacts didn't come from this specific cottage, but every single one of 'em came from some place just like it."

Tran shook his head, looking from the reverend to the historian. "Dinah Mae…"

Anders crossed his arms. "It's illegal to remove artifacts. No statutes about adding them. Do you think Thorne Marberger will bat an eye at running the Afters out of business with his resort hotel? This isn't just about a historical site. It's about saving the business owners and the very character of Possumwood."

He's not exactly wrong. But I can't condone chicanery, either. "You're pushing it, Reverend. You might be following the letter of the law, but the spirit? 'Not illegal' isn't the same as ethical. When did you say Dr. Cooper was coming?"

"Tomorrow," Dinah Mae frowned at the box of artifacts.

After the gift of the box, PC was inclined to cut Dinah Mae some slack, but she couldn't just let her off the hook. "Dinah Mae, I understand what you're trying to do. And I agree with you. In spirit. But you can't… fake a historical site. You, of all people, should understand that. Don't go creating your own Fiji Mermaid, even if there is a sucker born every minute."

Anders took his hat off and ran a hand through his thick, dark hair before putting the cap back on. "I hate it, but you're right. It just seems like we should be *doing* something, not waiting and hoping." He turned to Dinah Mae. "We need to work on our approach to Dr. Cooper tomorrow, figure out how we're going to convince her that the cottage needs to be restored and preserved."

"Agreed. Let's take this stuff back to the museum and we'll discuss it there."

They got in Anders' car and drove away.

"You okay, PC? You look a little shook up. Is it…?"

"The box. Yes. I don't want to talk about it right now."

Tran rattled his car keys in his pocket.

"You wanna grab a cup of coffee at the truck stop and talk about the case?"

"Sure."

PC yawned as Tran pulled onto 720. A mass of rubble loomed in the dark where the Best Southern Hotel used to stand. Hopefully, Renetta Sherman's *Purely Possumwood* boutique hotel project would work out. Anything was better than the stained stucco eyesore that had been the Best Southern.

The truck stop across the street didn't look especially busy. An *Under New Management* banner drooped above the front door. Tran parked, and they went inside. A server escorted them to a booth next to a spindly plastic Christmas tree, complete with fake presents, and took their order.

PC unrolled her silverware. "So, who do we know who is tall, can lift 250 pounds, and hated Whit Bulger?"

107

"Besides Steve Anders?"

"Or including. Here's another question. Do you think the cottage fire is related to Bulger's murder?"

Tran frowned and gave a slight shake of his head. "He was one of the first there, and you saw him leave."

"He did yell at somebody. Could be he saw something he wasn't supposed to see."

The cowbell on the door clanked. Ned Koehler and Tim Kowalski sauntered in.

Now here come two tall, muscular dudes. Wonder if Kowalski had a beef with Bulger?

PC looked at her companion. "Hey, Tran? What do you think the odds are that we can peel Koehler away from Kowalski for a few minutes to ask about his wife's music lessons with Bulger?"

"Probably good. He likes to talk. Let's let them order first, though."

"Good plan."

The waitress brought PC's fries and Tran's cherry pie, then left to seat the newcomers. They requested menus and took an agonizingly long time poring over them. PC was almost done with her food by the time they ordered.

Tran got to his feet and strolled over to their table. "Ned? Could we talk to you for a minute?"

"About?"

"Yesterday's drama."

Ned turned to Tim and exhaled loudly. "Be right back." He slid out of the booth to follow the officer.

Tran slid into his side of the booth and Koehler sat next to PC, his sinewy right forearm almost brushing hers. She scooted over a few inches. He had a fire and rescue emblem tattooed in red and black on the flat inner arm about midway between elbow and wrist. The artist had done an excellent job of making it look three dimensional.

The officer slid his empty pie plate out of the way. "Have you met Detective Donovan?"

Koehler gave Tran a flat smile and gave a slight tip of his cap to PC. "So, what do you need from me?"

PC twisted her neck to look at him. "That fire, huh? That was crazy."

"Yeah."

"Lucky you got there so quick. Seems like half the fire department was at the Christmas Tree lighting."

"I helped Beverly Miles set up her booth. Usually, she and my wife, Heidi, split a table, but Heidi's mother had surgery, so she went to take care of her. I left not too long after Bev was up and going. Had errands. The farm doesn't run itself. I was on my bike, so I could take some shortcuts gettin' around."

Tran's eyebrows shot up. "You ride a bike?"

Ned shrugged. "Yeah. When I can. Lot cheaper than buyin' gas for my super duty truck."

PC sipped her tea. "Ain't that the truth. I think it was so sweet that Mr. Bulger was giving singing lessons to Heidi so she could join the cantata."

"Yeah. Whit was a good guy. I love Heidi to death, but her singin' needed all the help it could get. Don't think Whit had an enemy in the world." Ned leaned toward Tran. "Do y'all have any leads on who killed him?"

PC turned a little more. "Nothing yet. Hey, you didn't happen to notice anything, did you when you arrived at the cottage? Any unusual people? An altercation someone had with Mr. Bulger?"

Ned shook his head. "No. The only thing was Makayla told me Paula Stein and her kids were inside. Paula's always been a good friend, and the thought they might have been killed in there…" He sighed.

Kowalski waved from across the dining room. A large basket of tortilla chips sat in the middle of the table, a bowl of queso dip next to it.

"Looks like the food's here." Ned stood. "Anything else?"

"No," Tran said. "Thanks Ned."

"Sure thing."

PC picked up a cold French fry and made a design in the scant pool of ketchup on her plate. "Not sure we're looking at a jealous husband."

When Tran pulled up at Rose's house, the detective was ready to relax and think about something other than Whit Bulger's murder.

PC unbuckled her seatbelt. "See you in the morning."

"Night."

PC trudged into the house. Rocky was sprawled on the couch under a crocheted blanket, watching TV. Cordite's nose poked out from under the afghan, then he jumped down from the sofa and stretched, taking a few stiff-legged steps toward his owner.

The detective leaned over and scratched behind his ears. "You keeping Rocky in line?" She straightened up and looked at her brother. "Thanks for feeding the animals, Rock."

"No problem. Mama's at Terry's. He's been doing some online cookin' class, and he's testin' out his new recipes on her."

PC chuckled. "You eat?"

"Yeah. Frozen dinner."

Unsatisfied by the greasy truck stop fries, she wanted something hot but was too tired to cook. And she'd just gotten home, so she didn't want to turn around and go back out. *Wonder if there's a can of soup in the pantry.*

The detective headed into the kitchen and rummaged through the canned goods. *Organic curried carrot soup. Sounds interesting. And quick.*

She opened the can, poured the contents into a bowl, and put it in the microwave. *What is soup without warm carbs?* PC popped some bread into the toaster. Cordite whined and wagged his tail.

"Fine. But be quick. I'm hungry." PC opened the doors to the back porch and the outside, checking for cats. "Coast is clear. Come on, Cordie."

The little dog trotted outside and down the steps. He made a beeline for his favorite tree.

The bottom fell out of PC's stomach.

The gate was open and there was not an ungulate to be seen. Please let Hazel and Arthur be in the back, away from the light. She trotted out to the pasture and called for them.

No joy. *Great. Rocky, you couldn't manage one simple thing?*

111

The dog was waiting for her on the back steps, shivering. PC opened the door and they both hurried into the house.

"Rocky? I need you to help me find the animals."

"What?"

"Did you close the gate with the chain and snap?"

He cleared his throat. "I might have forgot."

"The gate's open and they're all out. Let's go get 'em rounded up."

Rocky sighed and turned off the television. "I'll get my shoes." He groaned. "My phone's out of battery. Gimme a sec to put it on the charger."

"I'll grab some feed and halters. Meet you at the car."

He was leaning against the SUV when she got there with the equipment. PC put the animal wrangling supplies in the back, then got into the driver's seat.

Rocky sighed. "I'm real sorry about that. Didn't realize…"

She forced a calm she did not feel. "Not the end of the world. Let's just get them home before anything happens." PC shifted into reverse.

Rocky fidgeted with his seatbelt. "I have no idea where to even start lookin'."

"Don't worry. Gwen's as predictable as the sunrise. Pretty sure I know where to find her. Hope Arthur and Hazel tagged along."

PC pulled up in front of Truman Parker's house, a few blocks away. Guinevere had coveted his blue-ribbon roses for as long as the detective had known her.

"Rocky, get me that flashlight out of the glovebox, would you?"

He shifted his knees around so that he could open the compartment. "Here you go."

She got out of the car and shone the light around the yard, illuminating each fragrant bush. A raccoon dodged out of the spotlight, but there were no other quadrupeds to be seen.

PC got back in the car. "Okay. Next location."

"Where's that?"

"The Afters. She'll be *after* their rose hedge."

Should I tell Rocky about the box? PC almost missed a stop sign. If Rocky makes it through the end of the month, he'll be a full year sober. Daddy's death had knocked him for such a loop… He doesn't need a setback. I wish he could manage his emotions better, so I didn't have to.

Rocky barged into her reverie. "How's the case goin'?"

Why are you asking about this now? PC moved her arm over a little on the armrest. "Feel like I've made some progress, although it seems more like two steps forward and one step back."

"That's how it usually works, isn't it? I wasn't too well acquainted with Whit, but Mama's real shook up about it."

Oh. That *case.* The detective rolled to a stop at a traffic light before turning right. "Not surprised. I just wish she hadn't been the one to find the body."

"I know what you mean, sis. I know what you mean. Uh, shouldn't you have turned there on Crockett?"

"Well, I'm going the long way around so that we can drive past the front, east side, and the back. If we don't see them, we can go up the utility road on the west side."

"Got it. Speakin' of the west side… Have y'all caught the arsonist yet?"

"Not yet."

PC smiled to herself as she drove past Drew's house on South Cumberland. She turned right onto Main and passed *The Best Little Art Gallery in Texas*. As she came to its neighbor, *Vintage Glory Antiques*, she said, "Alright, Rock. Keep your eyes peeled for our fugitives."

She put on her flashers and drove slowly past the Afters' front entrance. No sign of the critters, so she turned right onto Crockett Street. All quiet on the eastern front. She was near the end of the block, about to turn onto 2nd Street, when she heard a long, low groan.

Rocky whipped his head toward PC. "What was that?"

She rolled down the windows. The groan was followed by a series of wheezing barks. Then a string of swear words.

"Uh-oh. I think we've found 'em, Rock. Sounds like someone else has, too. If they scared Arthur, Gwen's gonna have something to say about it."

The critters were not along the back of the Afters, so PC pulled up near the cottage. She handed her brother the flashlight and got the feed and halters from the car.

Rocky paused and sniffed the air. "Do you smell smoke?"

"Probably just the soot from the burned building." PC raised her head and breathed deeply. "You're right, though. It does smell more smokey than cindery."

Hoofers forgotten, PC approached the cottage. A glow came from the window in the living room side of the house.

She dropped the animal equipment and sprinted for her car. "Rocky! Call 9-1-1! The cottage is on fire!"

PC opened the liftgate to grab her fire extinguisher. Motion caught her eye and she whirled in time to see something crashing into the shrubbery across the street. It had a smooth round head and a slender, elongated snout. Its stocky arms were held in front of it as it ran into the bushes.

Adam Stein's corythosaurus.

PC let out her own stream of swear words. No time to go after him. She sprinted to the cottage, pulling the pin on the handle as she ran. The fire hadn't had a chance to consume much of the unspent fuel from the last time, and the detective was able to smother it through the open window with the small extinguisher. Rocky held the flashlight, but mostly spectated.

The detective turned to her brother. "Can you rattle the feed buckets and see if you can locate the animals? If the fire truck comes roaring up Code 3, I don't want them to bolt into traffic."

He nodded and picked up the accoutrements. "Arthur! Guinevere!" he called as he disappeared into the dark, trailing behind the bright flashlight beam.

Fire Chief Art Lopez, in his personal vehicle, was the first to arrive, followed closely by Tran.

"What happened?" the Chief asked.

"Mama's donkeys got out, and we were looking for them. Thought I heard Guinevere, so we got out of the car. Then I noticed the fire. I think I got it put out."

The three of them strode toward the cottage and eased inside, wary of any additional fire damage. Lopez inspected the foamy floor, then got on his radio and canceled the alarm.

"I did see someone."

Tran turned toward her. "Recognize them?"

PC shook her head. "Not in the dark. Tall, wearing a baseball cap. Dived into the bushes across the street. Doubt he's still there, but we should take a look."

They walked across the road, Tran's Maglite leading the way. They found a few broken branches in the wax myrtle hedge, but seemingly nothing else.

The officer had walked down the row of shrubs a few yards, leaving PC in shadow. "Hey, Tran. Need your light over here."

"Sorry." He turned around and the powerful beam fell on the olive-green leaves.

PC pointed to a branch just above one of the broken sections. "Look at this."

"Blood?"

"Yeah. It's smeared on the leaves so it's probably a contact transfer. He isn't bleeding heavily."

Blood is good, but DNA analysis takes time. Sure would have been nice if he'd dropped his hat, too.

"I've got a crime scene kit in my squad. Let's go grab some evidence bags."

"Y'all have to see this!" the fire chief shouted.

They rejoined Lopez in the cottage. He squatted near the deep burn in the floor by the window.

The Chief waved them over. "Take a look."

New gaps in the floor revealed globs of color.

Tran frowned. "What is that?"

Lopez straightened. "Looks like melted carpet. Let me get a pry bar out of my trunk."

"I'll get gloves." Tran walked with him toward the vehicles.

PC's guts turned to ice. There were not many reasons a person would stuff a rolled-up carpet under a building and set the place on fire.

The men returned and the chief got to work on the floorboards with the pry bar.

Tran handed PC a set of gloves. "Be right back. Gonna grab some of those bloody leaves across the street."

By the time he returned, enough of the wood was removed to pull up the object. Tran and Lopez hauled the roll of carpet up through the opening. Moving it over to a stable area of flooring, they carefully unrolled it.

The body of a petite blonde woman lay at the center of the rug, her long hair matted with dried blood.

Tran gasped. "Isn't that—"

"Heidi Koehler," Lopez finished his sentence.

Chapter 14

"WELL." PC BIT the inside of her cheek. "Guess Heidi's not at her sick mama's after all."

"Doesn't look like it." Tran reached for his phone. "I'll get Dr. Mack."

Lopez *tsked*. "Oh, Heidi. I am so sorry." He looked helplessly up at Tran and PC. "What's Ned going to do without her?"

PC returned his gaze. "You knew them well?"

"Yeah. I introduced them. I wouldn't exactly say there were two peas in a pod. It was more like night and day. Heads and tails. They were opposites, but you couldn't have one without the other. He was the big, tough guy, and she was the tiny, gentle woman. He carried her around on a silk pillow."

"What?" Tran asked, putting away his phone.

"Not an actual pillow." Lopez pursed his lips and his eyes fell back on Heidi. "What do you think happened?"

PC gestured to Heidi's head. "Based on the blood in her hair, probably blunt force trauma."

He scowled. "I can see that. I mean, why would someone hurt her?"

PC was torn between wanting to comfort him over the loss of his friend and needing to get information from him. "Ned told us earlier that her mother was sick, and Heidi traveled to visit her. Did she do that a lot?"

"Yes. Esmerelda has a heart condition. She just got a pacemaker put in. Heidi was staying with her to help out while she recovered. But yeah, Esmerelda's been in poor health for years."

Being told that her daughter's been murdered isn't going to help that.

PC studied the body. *No defensive wounds on the hands or arms. No ligature marks or bruising around the neck.* "Did Heidi have any siblings?"

"Yeah. Sister lives in Colorado Springs."

"And where does Esmerelda live?"

"Little north of Navasota."

PC shifted her eyes back to Lopez. "So, about half an hour away from Possumwood."

"Something like that."

Lopez's radio squeaked and chattered, and he turned away to reply.

A car door slammed outside. PC and Tran made their way to the cottage entrance.

Dr. Mack pulled a fishing tackle box out of his car. He hurried up the walkway, shaking his head. "No offense, PC, but murder seems to follow you around like a Hellhound. Where is she?"

Yeah. Tell me about it.

"Inside." Tran swept his arm toward the interior.

Officers Sanchez, Fusilier, and a male that PC didn't recognize arrived to process the scene.

Tran took his own photos and hastily scratched on his notepad before turning to PC. "I guess we should go find Ned."

"I guess so."

"Well, well, well. What is this?" Dr. Mack was examining Heidi's hair.

PC and Tran hurried over.

The detective looked over the ME's shoulder. "What is it?"

Dr. Mack frowned. "This dark stuff in her hair. It's not all blood. It's sticky, but it's viscous, not tacky." He stood up and wafted some air over the gloved hand with a smear of dark goo on his fingers. His nose wrinkled as he analyzed the aroma. "Seems to be… molasses? I'll have the lab test it."

It was PC's turn to frown. "Didn't you say Whit Bulger's body had traces of honey on it?"

"Yes. Yes he did."

The detective crossed her arms. "Honey… molasses. These things seem to be connected, but I don't see how. Do we have a confectionary killer? What's next? Maple syrup?

Tran widened his stance. "Any idea how long she's been dead?"

"Hard to say. It's been chilly, which has slowed the process down a bit. I doubt she died earlier than Thursday, though."

PC rubbed her forehead. "We should really go and inform her husband."

"Have you ever done a death notification, Tran?" PC gazed at the gas coachlight lamps flickering merrily on the front porch of Ned and Heidi Koehler's modern farmhouse.

"No."

"It doesn't get easier." She opened her door and got out of the squad.

They shuffled up the walk and onto the porch. PC sighed and rang the doorbell. Seconds ticked by. The curtain on the glass next to the door was pulled back. A moment later, the deadbolt turned.

Ned Koehler stood in the open doorway in a thick terrycloth bathrobe, looking puzzled. "Can I help you?"

PC waited a moment for Tran to say something, but he didn't. "May we come inside, please?"

"I guess." Ned slicked his wet hair off his forehead and moved out of the way.

The foyer opened to a great room that blended into an open-plan kitchen to the right. A dim floor lamp burned the near the couch, but the kitchen was brightly lit, and Ned bustled into it.

"Just got out of the shower, and I need to finish up the dishes," he said, picking up a tea towel. "Y'all got some questions about the fire, or is this a social call?"

PC took a deep breath. "Mr. Koehler, I think you should sit down."

His eyes shifted to Tran, who nodded.

Ned pulled out a stool from the granite breakfast bar, moving a large plastic tub of clear corn syrup out of his way. "For the bees. Gotta feed 'em in the winter. Okay. Y'all are makin' me nervous, here. What's up?"

Familiar words tumbled from PC's mouth. "Mr. Koehler, I regret to inform you that your wife has been murdered."

Ned blinked rapidly. His head started to shake. "No. There's been some mistake. She's at her mother's house."

Tran bit his lip. "I'm sorry, sir. She's not."

"You're wrong. I'll... I'll just call her." He stood to retrieve his phone.

"Mr. Koehler..." PC said softly.

He shook the device at her. "You're wrong and I'm gonna prove it." Ned tapped the screen. A short time later, he frowned. "It's gone to voice mail."

PC closed her eyes for a second. "Is there anyone we can call for you?"

"No." He whirled and flung his phone across the room, where it bounced off the sofa and onto a Persian rug. "No! This isn't real! Heidi...How? What happened?" His voice trailed into broken rubble.

The detective swallowed. "She was found at the burned cabin. Dr. Mack'll have some more information about the circumstances later."

Ned sank back onto the stool and buried his face in his arms that crossed on the counter. His back jerked unevenly as his breathing became ragged.

And if that wasn't bad enough, here comes an even worse part. "Mr. Koehler. I understand this is a terrible time, but I need to ask you a few questions."

"Now?" His voice was muffled by his arms.

"I'm afraid so. There's some information we need tonight, but perhaps you can come by the station in the morning and we'll take a more thorough statement from you."

Tran reached out and patted Ned's terry-covered forearm. The bereaved man's breath sizzled as he sucked it in rapidly. Both men jerked away from each other, and Ned's head popped up.

"Sorry," Tran mumbled.

PC swallowed the lump in her throat and took out her notebook. "Mr. Koehler, when did you last see your wife?"

"She left Thursday mornin'. That's when the hospital called and said her mama was there, and she was havin' surgery on Friday for the pacemaker."

"Have you spoken with her since then?"

Ned shook his head. "No. Cell reception out there's pretty hit or miss. She sent me a text yesterday, though. Said Esmerelda got through her surgery okay but she was real weak."

"What kind of vehicle was she driving?"

"Her blue Tacoma pickup truck. It's easy to spot—got signs for *Heidi's Honey* on the doors."

The detective nodded. "Do you know of anyone who might have wanted to hurt her, anyone with a grudge?"

Ned lowered his head until it drooped against his chest. "No. Everybody who knew Heidi loved her."

PC rubbed her head just behind her ear. "Are you sure there's no one we can call to come stay with you?"

"I'm sure."

The detective closed her notebook. "I'm sorry for your loss, Mr. Koehler. When you feel ready in the morning, come down to the station, and we'll talk some more."

He nodded.

Tran and PC showed themselves out. In the cruiser, Tran radioed the BOLO to dispatch, requesting officers to be on the lookout for a blue Tacoma truck with *Heidi's Honey* door magnets. Then he started the car.

PC let out a loud breath. "That's my absolute least favorite thing to do."

"Did that seem normal?"

"You'd be surprised how often they already know. Sometimes their loved one's involved with some sketchy people, and they half expect it, and sometimes, they just know. But denial is pretty common."

He pulled away from the curb. PC stared out the window into the night. Tran drove toward Rose's house in silence. PC didn't feel like talking and she was relieved he seemed to feel the same way.

Tsk. "What?" Tran grunted in exasperation.

PC looked up. The quickest route home would entail turning right onto County Road 12 at this T-intersection. However, construction barricades blocked their path. A new strip of concrete shone pale under the flashing yellow lights.

"Great," Tran muttered.

"Guess it's the scenic route."

Radio chatter bounced off PC's ears. She was replaying the death notification over and over in her mind. Were there any tells? Inconsistencies? Over/under reactions? Or were they genuine?

The spouse is always a person of interest, especially when the victim is female.

PC hoped they didn't encounter any loose cows or deer as Tran sped down the dark country roads and around Robinhood's barn to get back to town. At last, they came to 720. Home wasn't far away now. He slowed a little as the density of the buildings increased.

As soon as Tran turned onto Main Street, PC gasped.

"What's wrong?"

Chapter 15

PC CLAPPED HER hands to her cheeks. "I forgot all about Rocky. I left him trying to get Mama's critters back home."

"He's probably there by now." Tran changed lanes.

The detective shook her head. "I don't know about that. He's not very animal oriented."

"Why don't you call him?"

"He doesn't have his phone—put it in the charger before we left."

Tran slowed for a stoplight. "We're on the way to your house, anyway. I'm sure he'll be there. If not, we'll go find him. Okay?"

"Thanks."

A few minutes later, Tran pulled into Rose's driveway. PC got out and jogged across the yard. The gate to the livestock paddock was still agape.

Rocky, where are you?

The detective ran back to the squad. "He's not back."

"Where should we start?"

"I left them at the Afters."

"Then we'll start there."

Tran cruised slowly down 2ⁿᵈ street along the back of the Afters. All the law enforcement personnel in Mirabella County seemed to still be at the burned cottage. Even with the blue and red strobes, Rocky had her bright flashlight, so he should be easily visible, especially when they got back into the dark.

They might have hoofed it up the utility easement toward the park. "Go north on South Cumberland, then turn right on Main."

At the far end of City Park, almost obscured by the brightly lit Christmas tree, a ghost light danced among the bushes.

"I think I see him! Go up County Parkway."

Tran turned right and passed the courthouse before pulling into a slot at the park. He got out and scanned the darkness before he pulled his own flashlight. "I see what you mean."

"Rocky?" PC called as she hurried toward the glow.

"PC? 'Bout time you got here."

The pool of light from Tran's Maglite finally reached Rocky and beyond. Hazel lay in the grass, chewing her cud. Arthur paced back and forth between Hazel and Rocky. Guinevere stood, feet planted, leaning backward. A holiday wreath from one of the streetlights hung around her neck. Rocky had untied the ribbon from it and was vainly attempting to use it as a rope around the donkey's head. He also leaned backward, tugging fruitlessly on Gwen.

He looked over his shoulder at PC. "Sorry. I dropped the stuff you gave me. This is all I could find."

The detective ran her tongue over her teeth. "Alright. We'll figure it out."

He stopped pulling on Guinevere, and she stopped digging in her heels.

PC looked at the goat and the other donkey. "Tran? Can you put Hazel in the back of your car?"

He scowled. "I guess."

"Rock, put your belt around Arthur's neck like a rope. You and Tran get these two home, and I'll deal with Gwennie."

Hazel was apparently quite tired from her little excursion. She didn't put up too much fuss getting into the cruiser. Tran rolled down the windows, and PC wasn't sure if it was for her benefit or his. The goat stuck her head out and bleated a few times at PC as Tran slowly followed Rocky and Arthur down the street.

"Alrighty, then. What are we going to do with you?" PC said as she turned back to Guinevere.

But the donkey was gone.

PC sighed. *I really should have gotten my flashlight back from Rocky.* She listened carefully for hoofbeats as she swiveled her head slowly around.

There! Gwen's beige rump disappeared into the dark as she passed under a streetlight in front of City Hall. PC ran after her, and the donkey picked up her pace.

She trotted down Justice Avenue, right past the Possumwood Police Department, the detective jogging behind her. PC closed the distance, and Gwen broke into a lope. Without warning, she veered left and jumped the low wrought-iron fence that surrounded the graveyard next to Justice Lutheran Church. The detective had to go a little farther to reach the gate. She wasn't up to jumping hurdles tonight.

Gravel crunched under PC's feet as she strode down the narrow lane. She got her phone out and turned on the flashlight.

Better than nothing.

She was at the far end of the cemetery, at the U-bend of the road when she heard leaves rustling. PC hurried in that direction as fast as she dared in the dark. Soon she came upon Gwen, who was munching contentedly on a climbing rose covered in small red blooms that arced over a lichen-covered tombstone.

The detective stopped. A flash of metallic blue between the leaves caught her eye. Leaving the donkey to her snack for the moment, she walked to the other side of the bush.

A blue Tacoma pickup with *Heidi's Honey* signs was parked behind the shrubbery.

Her first thought was, I wonder if Reverend Steve Anders knows this is here. *Is that why he seemed flustered on the stage when someone yelled out 'Heidi's Honey' from the crowd?* Her second was that she'd better call Tran.

The speed of Guinevere's rose feast had slowed considerably by the time Tran arrived.

He handed PC a rope. "This what you wanted?"

She nodded and gestured toward the truck. "There's something that looks like blood in the bed. Didn't find the keys. They're probably with her phone in a dumpster somewhere."

The detective fashioned a makeshift halter with the rope and secured it around Gwen's head while Tran called in the location of the truck. When he got off the radio, she raised Gwen's lead. "I've got to get her home."

He waved, and she turned toward Rose's house. As she walked, PC looked around at the surrounding businesses.

Where could Heidi's killer have gone after he got out of the truck?

129

Justice Lutheran Church was immediately next door, and PC idly wondered if Reverend Anders had been kidding about needing gallons of molasses for gingerbread making.

The killer had taken advantage of everyone being at the tree lighting when he stashed the body under the caretaker's cottage— Adam Stein hadn't heard a monster crawling out from under the house, but one putting something under it. But why did the murderer set the house on fire *then*? If he'd come back after midnight, the place would probably have burned to the ground before anyone noticed, taking the body, and the Stein family, with it. Did he *want* Heidi to be found, or was he just a poor planner? He could easily have hidden the body, stashed the truck, and walked the few blocks from the cemetery to the park. No one would notice another person slipping into the crowd. Did he join the festivities and use the ceremony to establish his own alibi, or to implicate someone else?

Too many questions, not enough answers.

When PC returned with the petulant Guinevere, Rocky was waiting for her at the barn.

"What are you still doing out here?"

Her brother cleared his throat and rubbed his chin. "When I got home, I came in through the kitchen. Mama was unbuttonin' Terry's shirt and he was sayin' 'hurry, hurry.' I didn't..." he swallowed hard. "wanna interrupt nothin.'"

PC checked her FlitBit. Rocky had been at least twenty minutes ahead of her. "I'm going in the house."

She trudged toward the back porch, Rocky shuffling behind her. With the animals safely back in their pen, PC was more than ready to go inside. She was so tired, body and brain, she could barely even feel her feet, and her head felt like it was stuffed with oatmeal.

Rose stood by the floor lamp, her glasses on, poring over a small box.

Terry sat on the couch, shirt off, red welts on his skin glistening in the light. PC did a double take when she noticed a tattoo of a circus elephant in a pink and purple headdress on his upper right arm.

"Mama? What's going on?"

Rose spun toward her. "Oh, Primrose! Rocky! I'm so glad you're here. There's something wrong with that tea you bought yesterday."

"Oh?"

"I made us each a cup and stirred in some of that *Heidi's Honey*. Terry didn't get halfway through his before he broke out in hives."

Rocky's eyes widened. "Does he need to go to the hospital?"

"I'm fine," the patient chimed in. "Luckily, Rose had a full tube of hydrocortisone ointment and a bottle of antihistamine. Used to happen all the time, until I figured out I was allergic to sulfites."

PC tilted her head and looked from Terry to Rose. "Isn't that a preservative?"

"Yes. That's why I'm tryin' to find it on the label," Rose grumbled.

"Sulfur dioxide. Common in wine and dried fruit," Terry added. "Have to go out of my way to get sulfite-free wine. And don't get me started on dried apricots."

But it's probably not in dried herbs and tea. PC picked up the jar of dark buckwheat honey. "What about molasses?"

"That stuff is the devil! I can't have it at all."

PC set the jar down.

Of course. I know who the killer is, and just how to prove it.

Chapter 16

PC SAT IN her conference room office, staring at pictures of Whit Bulger and Heidi Koehler. Tran knocked on the door frame. "Ned's here."

Voices from the lobby carried down the hallway, coming into focus as they got closer.

A female voice. Sounded like Sanchez. "...sorry about your wife, Ned. Heidi was a beautiful person."

"She was," Ned answered.

"How did you hurt yourself?"

"It's nothing. Just a little burn from the fire on Saturday."

Sanchez led the bereaved into the conference room and gestured to a seat near PC. "Can I bring you anything to drink, Ned?"

"Some water would be nice."

Sanchez disappeared into the hallway. Tran sat down at the table across from PC and Ned. She studied the gauze wrapped around his right forearm. A few drops of blood had seeped through it. His left arm was plain and unblemished.

PC turned her chair to face Ned and scooted over until her knee was almost touching his. "Mr. Koehler—"

"Please. Call me Ned."

"Ned. Thank you for coming in. Again, I want to tell you how sorry I am for your loss."

"Thank you."

"Before we talk about Heidi, I'd like to ask you a few questions about Whit Bulger."

Tran's eyes got wider. Ned leaned back in his chair, away from the detective.

"Really?" Ned frowned. "I heard he fell. It was an accident."

PC shook her head. "No. It was murder. The killer staged it to look as if he'd fallen by breaking the safety rail and knocking over the hymnals."

"Now detective, sounds to me like you're just trying to make a murder out of a tragic accident. Not enough crime here for you?"

The detective held out her hands. "Then why didn't he scream?"

"Scream?"

"When he fell. Bart Hornsby was in the church all evening. My mother entered the sanctuary probably moments after it happened. But nobody heard a thing. It seems very odd that he would have fallen out of the choir loft and not let out so much as a croak of surprise. And of course, there was no thump. Even on that thick carpet, it would have made a noise."

"And what does that have to do with me?"

"Did you take the case of *Heidi's Honey* to the *Beverly's Beverages* booth at the tree lighting?"

"Yes. Heidi was out of town. Or at least, that's what I thought." He covered his face with his hands.

"And you're the one who broke the jar of honey in the shop?"

Ned looked up, frowning. "Is that a crime?"

"There was honey on Whit Bulger's body."

Ned's eyes narrowed but his lips curled into a pseudo-smile. "I'm the *only* person with access to honey in Possumwood? Really?"

"Let's have a look under your bandage."

Ned recoiled. "Why? It's just a burn. From the fire at the cottage? You may remember that, from when the person who murdered my wife tried to destroy her body?"

"It's interesting that you didn't have a burn yesterday, but you suddenly have one today. It's not a burn, is it? It's a donkey bite."

"That's absurd." Ned crossed his arms, the injured one closest to his body.

"No, it isn't. When you were re-lighting the fire at the cottage, you crossed paths with my mama's donkeys. You couldn't know Arthur is blind on his left side, or that Guinevere considers herself his protector. I've startled Arthur a time or two, and Gwen's bitten the fire out of me. I am well aware of what a donkey bite looks like."

"Fine." Ned lowered his head and glared at PC. "It's a donkey bite. I was just checking the cabin. Sometimes you think a fire's out, and it reignites hours later."

PC rubbed her forehead. "If that was true, you would have put it out, not run away. The killer had to be you, Ned. You killed Whit Bulger because he saw you trying to light the carpet after it failed to burn during the first fire at the cottage. You're the one he called out to."

Ned's head shook like a bobble head on a bumpy road.

"Did you text him? Call him? You lured him to the church and ambushed him. You don't have to answer that. Your phone records will show it."

Ned put his elbows on the conference table and covered his face with his hands. "I didn't know Paula and the kids were in the cottage. I swear!"

Probably true. Makayla said he looked upset when she'd told him. "You thought the fire would destroy Heidi's body, or at least make it impossible to identify, didn't you?"

"It was an accident. I never would have hurt her. Not on purpose. She fell and hit her head on the concrete fire pit."

PC let out a I'm-so-disappointed-in-you sigh. "Ned. If it was an accident, you would have called 9-1-1 to try to save the woman you loved. She was threatening to expose you, wasn't she?"

Ned laughed. "Expose me for what? Hitting the snooze button too many times in the morning?"

"Honey laundering."

"Money laundering? Are you serious?"

"No, Ned. *Honey* laundering. I didn't think much about it when Paula Stein said that Heidi could charm her bees into making double the expected amount of honey. But I couldn't figure out why Whit Bulger's body had honey on it and Heidi had molasses in her hair. Not until Terry had a reaction to the molasses in your dark allegedly buckwheat honey. And then I remembered the big bucket of corn syrup on your counter. You weren't using it to feed the bees, like you said. You were cutting the honey with corn syrup and molasses to double your production. Did Heidi find out, or did she just get tired of the scam?"

Ned's eyes glittered dangerously behind his narrowed lids. He picked at the tape on the bandage. "I want my lawyer."

Tran got to his feet and walked around the table. "Come on, Ned. Let's go."

Ned held his hands in front of him. "You gonna cuff me?"

"Do I need to?"

Ned bowed his head and shuffled off with Tran toward the holding cells.

PC walked back to her conference room office, tidied up the murder books of Whit Bulger and Heidi Koehler, and put them away. She stared at the cold case binders, trying to decide whether she had it in her to go through any of them today.

The old files had pulled PC back to the old cases, one in particular. One supposedly solved homicide. She had to find out who was at the party where Clem Wilson was murdered.

Tran finally came back into the room.

She turned away from the shelf. "Where's Woody? I need to talk to him."

Tran frowned. "You didn't hear?"

"Hear what?"

"They took him to hospice yesterday."

Chapter 17

"Hospice?" The word was a kick to PC's gut.

Tran shook his head. "He didn't want you to know how bad it was. But I thought… someone would have said something."

PC's head was shaking on its own, and she didn't seem to be able to stop it. "I knew he was sick. But I didn't think… I thought he was going to recover."

"You remember back in February, when the Valentine's buffet got poisoned, and he ended up in the hospital?"

"How could I forget?" She remembered Dr. Mack telling her this not so long ago. She struggled with what to say, so she just let Tran talk.

"Well, that's when they found the cancer. Stage four. They gave him six months to a year. Looks like he's gonna split the difference." Tran smiled bitterly. "The chemo wasn't too bad for him, at first, but it seemed like the damage just built up. He got more and more treatments, but the cancer just kept spreading."

"I have to see him."

Tran drove them out to Azalea Manor. The nursing home seemed miles and miles away. When they finally arrived, PC stumbled across the over-sized gravel of the parking lot and flung open the door. She jogged down the hall toward the front desk, dodging a man with a walker. The sound of crying got louder as she approached.

Durelle Fennec, the nursing home director, was holding Hilda Wilson in her arms. Hilda's body shook with great wracking sobs. The door to one of the patient rooms stood open, and Officer Charles Bourgeois stood just inside. PC pushed past him.

Inside, a nurse was disconnecting Woody from the various monitoring devices. The IV had already been pulled from his arm.

No.

She stumbled toward the bed. The chief's eyes were closed. His chest did not rise. PC knew what dead looked like. Hot tears streamed down her face.

Why him? Why?

The detective squeezed his still warm hand. "Godspeed, Woody. Godspeed," she whispered, her eyes closed. Swallowing hard, she wiped her eyes, then left the room.

Hilda, eyes red and puffy, turned to PC. She looked so fragile that the detective was almost afraid to touch her. The older woman held out her arms and PC enfolded her in a close embrace. "I'm so sorry, Hilda."

That prompted a new round of sobbing. When she finally got hold of herself, she let PC go. Her voice hoarse with tears, she said, "I'm glad you came."

Rose appeared from out of nowhere and threw her arms around Hilda. PC turned to see her brother standing there with his hands in his pockets.

She took his arm and led him away from the two women. "Why didn't you tell me?"

Rocky held up his hands. "I didn't know. I was off yesterday, remember? Ms. Fennec called and told me what happened, said I needed to bring Mama to see Hilda."

Tran stood next to Bourgeois, silently watching the nurse until she slipped out of the room, leaving them to say their goodbyes.

PC looked out the window in Phineas Scott's office. Anubis, his Mexican Hairless dog, glared disapprovingly at her.

Scott cleared his throat. "Of course, this is very awkward timing, and if it could wait, I would let it. The Police Chief position is not one that can stay open indefinitely."

"What's that got to do with me?"

"Possumwood needs you. You've got the experience to run the department. More than enough experience."

"Except that I'm retired."

"You can un-retire."

PC shook her head. "Phineas, Woody's mother hasn't even finished making the funeral arrangements for him. This just doesn't feel right."

"I agree. Do you think I want this? Woody's going to be tough to replace. But you… you grew up here. You know Possumwood like the back of your hand. I need someone like that. I need you."

PC rubbed her forehead and pinched the bridge of her nose. "I've been away from Possumwood twice as long as I ever lived here. I think you need someone with a more recent resume."

"Don't make me beg."

The front door of the Possumwood Police Department seemed unusually dull. Might just have been the overcast sky muting the colors of the world. PC pushed it open and found Annie on front desk duty.

The dispatcher's somber eyes lingered on PC. "He's waiting for you."

The detective stepped through the security door. She spared a glance at the conference room that had been her makeshift office for most of the past year and kept going to the chief's office.

It was just like Woody had left it. Cracked faux leather and chrome visitors' chairs that looked like they'd escaped from the 1970s. Probably had. Heavy oak desk with a calendar pad taking up most of the center. She ran a finger over the blue glass paperweight.

"He got that from his mom." Tran had come into the room, file folder in hand.

"So, how does it feel?"

He sat behind the desk, setting the folder to the side. "Weird. I mean, it's something I had aspired to, but I didn't want it... like this."

"I'm sure you'll do just fine, Chief Tran." PC smiled at him. "And I'm only a phone call away, if you need any help."

"I appreciate that more than you realize." He opened the center drawer and took out an envelope.

"Woody left this for you."

"For me?"

Detective Sergeant PC Donovan was printed in bold letters on the cream-colored paper. She sat in the Naugahyde chair and opened the letter.

Dear Rosie:

I'm sorry. I really wanted to tell you in person, but I ran out of time. Or nerve. Sorry for that, too. I started writing this back in March, after I found out about the cancer. I wanted to get everything down and organized before I told you. But it never seemed like the right time.

The whole thing was an accident. My mom had bought the Colt Python for protection. I borrowed it sometimes. Don't believe she had any idea. We practiced shooting tin cans out in the woods.

Clem, Whit Bulger, and I played pool a lot. We could usually find some—let's face it—marks over in Horice. That's where Whit was from. They never thought kids were going to be a threat. Man, were they wrong. We usually made a good chunk of change at Mickey's Pool Hall. But for whatever reason, nobody was coming out to shoot pool that week. It was mostly just the three of us, and I couldn't make any money like that.

You have to understand. My mom was in a bad spot. She tried to hide a lot of stuff from me, but I overheard her on the phone, talking to my aunt. She was going to lose the house if she didn't come up with the mortgage in three days.

I didn't know what else to do. I am so sorry. I had to break things off, because I just couldn't face you, knowing what I had planned. The Homecoming Dance was just real bad timing. I was too young and dumb to think there might have been another way. I should never have listened to Clem.

I'm not proud of what I did, but I hope that one day you can forgive me. I didn't think the gun was loaded. But that's on me. You ALWAYS assume the gun is loaded, right?

There must have been a round chambered. I didn't check. I just thought we were going to scare him, not hurt him.

Even though we all wore masks when we entered to the ShopStop that night, Mr. Donovan could tell who we were. I pulled the gun and told him to put all the money in a plastic bag. I tried to disguise my voice, but he recognized me. He told me he'd have helped, if I'd just asked. I didn't want the money anymore, not like that. I have never been so ashamed of myself in my entire life.

When I lowered the gun, Clem grabbed it. Your dad was trying to talk him down. Whit and I started dragging Clem out. That's when a gun went off. I was aware Mr. Donovan kept a .357 under the counter, and I thought he was shooting at us.

We let go of Clem and ran. When I stopped to open the door, I could see my cousin prying open the cash register. And your dad, laying across the counter.

Clem came out with the money and that black and white box, got in the car, and floored it all the way to Horice. We only got to Mickey's a little later than usual, so nobody noticed.

We split the money three ways. I added it to the little bit I'd been able to shark at pool, and we didn't get thrown out of the house that month. I had decided to go to the sheriff and come clean when Clem said he was real worried my mother might have a terrible accident at home, all alone, if I wasn't there to protect her.

After graduation, I just drifted for a year. Had trouble figuring out what to do. Couldn't live with myself, but I couldn't end it, either. Who would take care of Mama? She deserved better than me, that's for sure, but I was all she had.

Summer Langborn, a friend of Whit's, lived in one of the fancy new houses in Whispering Oaks. Her parents were in Europe for a week, so she decided to throw a party. That was the same week the sheriff announced that they'd gotten a donation big enough to double the reward money for turning in your dad's murderer.

After everything he was holding over me, I heard Clem telling some girl that he thought he knew who the killer was, and once he collected the reward money, he was going to buy a fancy new truck. Asked if she'd go for a ride with him.

I was so mad I couldn't see straight. I told Whit and we pulled Clem into the utility room to have a little discussion. He said he was just kidding around, but Whit and I were furious. Clem reached behind his back and Whit jumped him. I caught glimpses of the gun as they struggled. The music in the living room was so loud nobody even heard the gunshot. Whit got up. Clem didn't.

Summer just happened to come in and saw Whit all bloody and Clem on the floor. She screamed and ran out. If they tested the ballistics on the gun, it would lead back to me and Whit, so while he waited for the cops, I grabbed the gun and ran down the street to some new construction.

They had a frame and some rebar laid out to pour the driveways of several houses. I picked one and buried the gun in the sand. I was sure nobody'd ever find it. But Fate had other ideas.

Guilt ate me up. But I couldn't turn myself in. What would happen to my mother if I got sent to prison? So, I kept my trap shut.

The only thing I could do was try to make up for it. I became a cop. Protecting Possumwood and keeping my secret. I was so good at pretending that I almost forgot what I'd done. Then you came to town, and it was all fresh again.

I know I don't deserve it, but all I really want is your forgiveness.

Have a good life.

Woody

A tear trickled down PC's cheek. Then another. And another. Now she knew. And she wished she didn't.

Tran's brow crinkled. "You okay?"

"No." The detective stuffed the letter back into the envelope. "But I will be."

Chapter 18

PC OPENED THE ornate black and white box that Dinah Mae Brown had given her. She remembered the day her father had returned from his month-long business trip. His suitcase was a veritable Santa sack stuffed with presents and treats from a place so far away PC had trouble imagining it.

Daddy had said the box was very old. She had marveled at its intricate design then, wondering how anyone could have figured out how to make such an amazing thing, especially hundreds of years ago.

Now she couldn't stand the sight of it.

The detective tucked Woody's letter inside and snapped the container shut. She had almost burned the note but couldn't bring herself to destroy the guilt-soaked pages. She knew the secret now, and perhaps knowing was enough to stop Death from dogging her every step. PC had felt a weight lift off her shoulders when she was able to close the book on Trey Donovan's murder. Even if she was the only person who would ever know the truth.

She shoved the box deep under her bed. Perhaps she'd take it back to her house in Houston. Rose should never set eyes on it. Rocky, either, for that matter. Sometimes knowing is worse than not knowing.

She took Cordite out for a final potty break before hitting the hay. While he sniffed out the perfect puddle place, PC leaned on the three-rail fence that separated the livestock from the back yard.

Hazel lay near the water trough, chewing her cud. Guinevere and Arthur picked at the last of the hay. None seemed any the worse for wear after their downtown misadventure.

"What would you do without me?" she asked the contented critters.

More like what would Mama do without me. Even with, or maybe especially with, Rocky's help, she'd never be able to corral the cunning Gwen when her wanderlust went wild. Particularly if she led her pasture mates on a promenade around town. Not to mention the terrible scare they'd had when Rose had gone out to commune with the quadrupeds by herself and fallen, spending hours laying in the cold rain.

Grass flew as the dog scratched the ground, scattering *eau du Cordite* to put any interlopers on notice.

"Come on, it's cold out here. Let's go back inside."

PC brushed her teeth and Cordie burrowed under the comforter. He didn't have much time to warm the sheets before the detective slipped under the covers and turned out the light.

The orange glow that seeped into PC's window from the streetlight on Travis was just bright enough that the patterns in the textured ceiling seemed to slither and swirl in the mostly dark room. She closed her eyes to avoid the eeriness.

And then she was standing in front of a bin of fresh peaches. The sweet tangy smell brought a rush of saliva to her mouth. She picked one up, the fuzzy fruit firm in her hand.

"*Buenos dias.*"

PC dropped the perfect peach, her whole body tensing. She looked up at her fellow shopper, a Hispanic man in his late twenties. She recognized him from his profile. Jorge Ramirez. Gunshot victim. She braced herself for the gruesome display as he turned his head to reveal the lethal wound.

But he just smiled at her, whole and happy.

She looked around the store for other people. Elma Carpenter leaned on her walking frame, a small basket of produce in front of her. But the thirty-seven stab wounds she had when PC had last laid eyes on her were gone. And so it went. She recognized every shopper, every stocker. And they were perfect. The detective covered her mouth with her hand. Then she noticed her own basket was full of fresh peaches and she felt it was time to check out.

PC wove through the aisles to the register. She nearly dropped her basket when she saw the cashier.

"Daddy?"

He beamed at her and nodded before he picked up the first peach to scan it.

"Thank you, Rosie. You solved it after all this time." He scanned another peach.

PC frowned. "But Daddy. I can't tell anyone."

"I know. But now you can let it go. This case has been haunting you for decades. *I've* been haunting you for decades. And now, it's finished."

The detective felt a tear on her cheek. "Does this mean you're happy to cut ties with me?"

He stopped scanning peaches. "Rosie. Baby. Of course not. That's not it at all. My murder was like a ball and chain around your ankle, dragging you down. Now you're free. I'm free, too. I tell you what. Any time you want to talk, we can meet up here. Even if your brain doesn't remember it when you wake up, your heart will." He handed her the grocery bag filled with peaches.

She reached for it and touched his hand. The store exploded into a light so bright she closed her eyes. The brilliance that filled her heart was like a distillation of all the goodness from home-baked cookies and Christmas mornings, mother's kisses and father's bedtime story readings. Just when she felt her heart was so full it must surely burst, the light faded and she slipped into a deep sleep.

Cordite woke her before her alarm with his patented I-really-have-to-pee whine.

"Really? You couldn't wait another..." she checked her FlitBit. "Twelve minutes?"

He whined again.

PC dressed quickly and strode toward the back porch. In the kitchen, one of the under-cabinet lights was on, and the detective stopped as if she'd run into a glass wall.

In the pool of brightness sat a large, flawlessly ripe peach.

When she could move again, she picked it up. "Thank you, Daddy."

If there was a more perfect Christmas gift, she didn't know what it was.

❄ ❄ ❄

PC pulled into a parking space at the Justice Avenue Baptist Church. The singers were arriving early to prepare for their performance, and eager spectators had already begun to trickle in, hoping to scoop up the best seats.

"Mama? Terry? You ready?"

"Oh, honey," Rose said from the passenger seat. "I'm as ready as I'm gonna get."

"Me too, my darling," Terry added from the back seat, where he was squeezed in between Rocky and Drew.

"Hopefully, the weather holds and we don't have to leave early." PC zipped her coat and got out of the car.

The five of them headed for the entrance. The ten-foot Jesus fountain was surrounded by scarlet-blooming poinsettias. A colored floodlight tinted the water green. A man in a brown Christmas pageant robe huddled in the corner, out of the biting wind, taking a cigarette break. Each glass entryway was decked with a fresh evergreen wreath, trimmed with a red velvet bow and sprays of golden berries.

Drew opened the door, and they entered the lobby. A goat bleated. The animal wrangler for the living nativity scene faced away from them, struggling to get a goat into the small pen with a donkey and a very fluffy goat, who were already munching hay from a manger.

That donkey looks familiar. Don't remember which one was Christine and which was Jelly, though.

Mary stood talking on her cell phone while the Baby Jesus doll dangled by one leg from her grasp. *Must have been Joseph outside.*

Rocky patted his belly. "I need to make a pit stop. Be right back." He left in search of the men's room.

The livestock supervisor turned around.

"Hey, Justice!" Rose called out.

"Hey, yourself." She gave up tugging on the goat and just scooped it up in her arms. "I'm lookin' forward to seein' the show."

"Thanks, honey."

The Donovan party stepped into the sanctuary. Rose and Terry entered the chancel and climbed the stairs to the choir loft to take their places and warm up.

PC and Drew found seats in the center section, tenth row. Four Christmas trees, decorated with white lights and red ornaments graced the performance area behind the pulpits. Two taller trees, one on either side of the altar, twinkled underneath the loft. The two smaller trees flanked them, a few feet away.

Fresh evergreen garland, twined with tiny LED lights, covered the communion rails and the recently repaired safety railing of the choir loft. Lush poinsettias clustered in front of each of the two pulpits.

A woman struggled down the aisle, carrying two garment bags and a box overflowing with out-sized Christmas presents, and PC felt for just a moment she was in the opening scene of *The Nutcracker*.

Drew stood up. "Let me help you."

The woman turned. "That'd be great. Thanks."

"Mary Anne?"

"Hey there, PC!"

Drew took the box and continued toward the chancel.

Mary Anne McDonald folded the clothes over her arm. "It's good to see you. Haven't been to darts in forever—this cantata. Hope you enjoy it. Gotta go show Drew where to put those props."

She turned and hurried away.

A few minutes later, Drew returned and sat next to PC on her left.

He had barely settled in when Rocky slipped into the chair next to her on the right.

"Hey, y'all!"

The three of them twisted in their seats to see Daisy waving from the top of the aisle, a long black pack slung across her body. She was accompanied by a young man.

Zachary must be home from school.

PC's sister and nephew came to sit with them. Daisy unzipped the long canvas bag and pulled out a camera tripod.

"What are you doing, Dais?" PC asked as she dodged an unfolding leg.

"What does it look like? I'm gonna record Mama and Tyson singin'."

Drew leaned forward. "The church has a professional videographer recording it. If I remember correctly, they're livestreaming it, but when it's over, you can watch the replay any time."

Daisy pouted.

A group of five people sat in row nine, directly in front of Daisy's tripod, blocking her phone's view of the stage.

She sighed and began to put away her equipment. "Just as well, I guess."

As they sat and chatted, the seats filled. PC recognized many of the faces and hoped she would get the opportunity to visit with her Possumwood friends over refreshments at the end of the show.

At long last, Reverend Richard Costas stepped out from the organist's alcove, mic in hand.

"Good evening, ladies and gentlemen! Welcome to our Christmas cantata."

The singers outdid themselves. The Possumwood Players community theatre performed skits in between songs, so it was almost like a musical. Except instead of actors bursting into song, songs paused for the acting. PC turned the brightness on her phone down as low as she could and checked the weather from time to time.

An hour and a half later, performers and spectators alike spilled into the fellowship hall to talk and enjoy refreshments. As Reverend Anders had promised, Justice Avenue Lutheran Church had provided a table filled with various species of gingerbread: decorated cookies, cupcakes, and slabs of loaf, drizzled in white glaze.

Another table featured ginger ale punch with a ring of frozen raspberries floating in the middle. Yet another table held cheese, crackers, crudites, chips, and dip.

Three-quarters of an hour passed. PC stepped outside to check the weather and use her phone to view the radar. A big pink blob was approaching, and the wintry mix should arrive in the next thirty minutes.

She stepped back into the gathering and showed Drew the radar projection.

"Mama? Terry? That weather's coming in. We should probably get going."

Rocky was easy to round up, but it took an additional fifteen minutes of good-byeing to get Rose and Terry out the door.

Something cold and wet hit PC's cheek. She looked up. Under the glare of the parking lot lights, she could see big, wet globs of snow, falling slowly and shattering silently on the asphalt and melting away.

"Well, I'll be!" Rose paused. "It's snowin'!"

"Don't look like it's stickin', though," Rocky pointed out.

PC clicked the remote to unlock the doors. "Yeah, but there's a cold front behind it, so it might. We should get home before that happens. I don't want to be out here when the water on the road starts to freeze."

As she drove, she had to turn the wipers on, as the slushy white stuff fell harder. By the time they made it back to Rose's house, the big, wet clumps had given way to smaller, lighter flakes that danced in the icy wind.

"Drew, can you help get everyone inside? I'm going to check on the animals."

"Of course."

"I'll get some hot chocolate on." Rose grinned.

PC hurried out to the barn and gave Hazel, Gwen, and Arthur more hay. They were sheltered from the wind and precipitation, and none were shivering. She'd check on them again before she went to bed.

A beige blur flashed by in the yard. Drew stood on the back steps, silhouetted by the dim porch light, and Cordite raced around the yard like a maniac.

"How'd he convince you to let him out?" PC was almost to the stairs.

"Had dogs most of my life. Still speak the language."

The detective stood next to Drew on the wide top step, protected from the snowfall by the eave, and they watched the little dog tear around.

"I miss having a pup."

PC turned toward Drew. "Why don't you get one? There's that *Just Paws* rescue in town—I saw them at the hardware store doing adoptions."

"Not sure I want a puppy. I was thinking an older dog that's already trained. Small, like twenty-five pounds or so."

PC raised an eyebrow. "You could be describing Cordite."

"Huh."

At last, the dog's excitement was spent. He slowed to a trot, then stopped to add his own precipitation to his favorite oak tree before loping back to the steps, tongue lolling from his mouth.

"Come on, you nut." PC opened the door and the three of them stepped onto the screened porch.

Drew looked toward the ceiling. "What's that?"

PC's eyes followed his. "Oh." She raised an eyebrow. "Who on earth would think to put mistletoe there?"

"Who indeed?" Drew lifted PC's jaw with his fingers and bent to kiss her.

This time, she didn't pull away.

If you enjoyed this book, please consider leaving a review at your favorite book site. Reviews help other readers find and enjoy new books!

Other books by Holly Dey:

Manor of Death: The Possumwood Mysteries Book 1

Death on the Half Shell: The Possumwood Mysteries Book 2

Azalea Trail of Death: The Possumwood Mysteries Book 3

Death Re-Enacted: The Possumwood Mysteries Book 4

Death Rides a Bobcat: The Possumwood Mysteries Book 5

Key to Death: The Possumwood Mysteries Book 6

Death Curated: The Possumwood Mysteries Book 7

Pool of Death: The Possumwood Mysteries Book 8

All Death No Cattle: The Possumwood Mysteries Book 9

Death is Lager than Life: The Possumwood Mysteries Book 10

Art of Death: The Possumwood Mysteries Book 11

Little Town of Death-Lehem: The Possumwood Mysteries Book 12

Winter: Boxset Collection Books 1-3

Spring: Boxset Collection Books 4-6

Summer: Boxset Collection Books 7-9

Fall: Boxset Collection Books 10-12

Large Print Editions

Manor of Death: The Possumwood Mysteries Large Print Edition Book 1

Death on the Half Shell: The Possumwood Mysteries Large Print Edition Book 2

Azalea Trail of Death: The Possumwood Mysteries Large Print Edition Book 3

Death Re-Enacted: The Possumwood Mysteries Large Print Edition Book 4

Death Rides a Bobcat: The Possumwood Mysteries Large Print Edition Book 5

Key to Death: The Possumwood Mysteries Large Print Edition Book 6

Death Curated: The Possumwood Mysteries Large Print Edition Book 7

Pool of Death: The Possumwood Mysteries Large Print Edition Book 8

All Death No Cattle: The Possumwood Mysteries Large Print Edition Book 9

Death is Lager than Life: The Possumwood Mysteries Large Print Edition Book 10

Art of Death: The Possumwood Mysteries Large Print Edition Book 11

Little Town of Death-Lehem: The Possumwood Mysteries Large Print Edition Book 12